LIKE
NOTHING
AMAZING
EVER
HAPPENED

ALSO BY EMILY BLEJWAS

Once You Know This

The Story of Alabama in Fourteen Foods

LIKE NOTHING AMAZING EVER HAPPENED

EMILY BLEJWAS

DELACORTE PRESS

Text copyright © 2020 by Emily Blejwas
Jacket art copyright © 2020 by Dan Burgess

All rights reserved. Published in the United States by Delacorte Press, an imprint of Random House Children's Books, a division of Penguin Random House LLC, New York.

Delacorte Press is a registered trademark and the colophon is a trademark of Penguin Random House LLC.

Visit us on the Web! rhcbooks.com

Educators and librarians, for a variety of teaching tools, visit us at RHTeachersLibrarians.com

Library of Congress Cataloging-in-Publication Data
Names: Blejwas, Emily, author.
Title: Like nothing amazing ever happened / Emily Blejwas.
Description: First edition. | New York : Delacorte Press, [2020] | Summary: In small-town Wicapi, Minnesota, in 1991, twelve-year-old Justin struggles to pick up the pieces of his life after the unexpected death of his father.
Identifiers: LCCN 2018060961 | ISBN 978-1-9848-4848-2 (hc)
ISBN 978-1-9848-4849-9 (glb) | ISBN 978-1-9848-4850-5 (ebook)
Subjects: | CYAC: Junior high schools—Fiction. | Schools—Fiction. | Community life—Minnesota—Fiction. | Single-parent families—Fiction. | Death—Fiction. Minnesota—Fiction.
Classification: LCC PZ7.1.B627 Lik 2020 | DDC [Fic]—dc23

The text of this book is set in 12-point Life LT.
Interior design by Ken Crossland

Printed in the United States of America
10 9 8 7 6 5 4 3 2 1
First Edition

TO MINNESOTA, WITH GRATITUDE

But in a story, which is a kind of dreaming,
the dead sometimes smile and sit up
and return to the world.

—Tim O'Brien,
The Things They Carried

CHAPTER ONE

"When you live in a place where nothing ever happens, you have to make something happen." That was my brother talking, after the police busted him and his friends for TPing the Hornet hockey captain's house when we beat Edina last fall. He was smiling when he said it because Murphy's always smiling. And he has the smile of a million lightbulbs. "Dazzling" is the word, if you're into words. His smile works wonders on everyone. His teachers. Pastor Steve. The cops that let him and most of the starters off with a warning and probably a laugh and a thump on the back. And on Mom, but not on that day. "Do you know the last time we beat Edina in the opening game?" Murphy asked. "In 1978! Justin wasn't even born!"

"Yes, I was," I said. "I was born in May, dummy." The memory gets a little darker then, like a cloud passed over it and shadowed our little kitchen table surrounded by wallpaper with both flowers and stripes. It always bugged me. "Just decide," I told the walls once, while chewing my Frosted Flakes. "Flowers or stripes." Murphy was downing an egg sandwich in three bites and grinning and filling the kitchen with sunbeams and said, "So serious, Little Monk!" Then he drank whatever orange juice was left in the carton, grabbed his backpack, and ran out the door before Mom could make him drive me to school.

Even with the cloud and shadow, I do remember Mom threatening to take the car away and Murphy running both hands through his hair, but I don't remember if she actually took the car away. I remember the cat jumping onto the table and Murphy picking her up and doing her voice to Mom. "Meow, Judith. Where's your team spirit? Meow. Do you need to join the booster club? Rah, rah, rah!" He pumped Axl Rose's little paw in the air. And I remember Mom turning to Dad and saying, "Larry. A little help?"

And Dad said, "Cake eaters." Then Mom must have thrown both hands up, and Murphy must have flashed his sunshine smile, but all I remember is Dad. The words he said aren't important. Everyone knows we call Edina "cake eaters." It's something about them being richer than us, even though Minnetonka's got plenty of rich kids. What's important, if you're trying to figure out my dad, is that those two words were all he said. The entire night. Sometimes he'd go a whole day only saying ten words and sometimes he got by with zero. Zero words!

If Murphy remembers saying "When you live in a place where nothing ever happens, you have to make something happen," he would take it back in a millisecond. We all would. We would all give anything to go back to living in a place where nothing ever happens.

．．．

"They should cancel school on days like this," Mom says. "It's not safe."

I pull my scarf down. "Good idea. Want to write me a note?"

She smiles, but her eyes are so sad they cancel it out. Like an x on both sides of the equation. "You've missed too much already," she says. I nod and pull my scarf back up. I have missed *a lot* of school.

In the apartment hall, I used to land hard on the bottom step to see how loud I could make it squeak, but for some reason now that squeak makes my stomach roll over itself like the mealworms in Mr. Bauer's room when you poke them with a pencil. I jump over the step completely and push through the door and into the gray wind.

"This is the worst it gets," Mom likes to tell herself in February. Because would you believe she grew up in Florida? She actually *lived* in the place where we all want to be all the time. Where the cake eaters go for spring break and come back with tans and bleached hair and coral necklaces and neon shirts with names of islands on them. And the rest of us are still pasty little fish swimming in the same drab pond, now with a bunch of tropical fish mixed in to make us feel bad.

"You must've really loved Dad to move to Minnesota," I told Mom once, and she smiled. "I did," she said. "I do." She did/does too. Even though he woke up screaming sometimes, or Mom woke up drenched because Dad sweat buckets in the sheets. There was something about Dad that made her love him through all that and lots more. There was something good about Dad that was indestructible. That came before Murphy and me. The Dad we never knew. Never would. Never will. What's the right verb now? I should ask Mrs. Peterson. Ha ha.

My head's down against the wind, but I can see the comic shop corner out of the tops of my eyes, and I swear if Phuc isn't standing outside I'm leaving without him. It's too cold to slow down. I already can't feel my toes, and I'm only two blocks from the apartment. I watch my boots scrape across the ice and salt until I get to the corner. My eyes are watering and the water is freezing in my eyelashes. "Hey," Phuc says, muffled by his scarf. I nod at him and we walk without talking because our mouths are full of spit and wool.

At the next corner we wait for the bus, silent on the outside, but sometimes the cold is so strong, it feels like a sound. Like a siren going off in your head, high-pitched. Kind of like the one Wicapi runs at noon on the third Wednesday of every month, just to make sure everything's okay. Dad died on a Tuesday night, and that siren ran the next day and I thought, *You have got to be kidding me. Everything is not okay.*

. . .

The heart-o-gram girls set up a table front and center inside the main doors. As usual, they're all wearing red or pink sweaters and red or pink nail polish. As usual, they have a massive glittery box that will be stuffed with heart-o-grams for all the popular kids by Valentine's Day. But this year they convinced a bunch of hockey players to pass out flyers too, so you have no chance of avoiding them. "Hey," a huge blond kid says to me, and shoves a flyer in my hand. "Buy a heart-o-gram. Only a dollar."

Phuc and I turn the corner, out of sight of the hockey players and heart-o-gram girls, and Mitchell passes by and jabs me in the ribs with one finger. "Loser," he says, but without any emotion, like it's just a fact. The way oxygen is the eighth element on the periodic table. "It seems like oxygen should be first," someone told Mr. Bauer, but he frowned at us and said not all of science is about humans.

Phuc doesn't notice Mitchell. He's reading his flyer. "I can think of twenty-five hundred things I'd rather spend a dollar on," he says, and crumples the paper into a ball.

"Like what?"

"Um. A hot dog. Twenty gumballs. Two Butter-fingers. A pack of Star Trek cards."

"Great. Only 2,496 more to go," I tell him. We get to our lockers and spin the dials and shove all our winter stuff into the bottom, where it will thaw and make a puddle by the end of first period.

"What? Like you're gonna send a heart-o-gram?" Phuc asks. "Or are you? Are you finally gonna tell Jenni-with-an-*i* about your undying love for her?" He's moving his head around in front of a tiny mirror stuck to the inside of his locker, making sure his hat didn't mess up his hair gel. I told him gelling his hair straight up is not the best strategy for staying under the radar, and he said, "I'm the only Vietnamese kid at this whole school. People still say my name like the F word even though I've been here since second grade. I'll never be under the radar." And I couldn't really argue with that. (His name is pronounced *Foc,* by the way. Ridiculously easy.)

"I'm not in love with Jenni-with-an-*i*," I say.

Phuc nods once at himself in the mirror and slams his locker. "Whatever you say. See you in third." He walks away, and then calls back, "I'll spot you a dollar if you need it!" Some girls passing by give me sticker smiles like maybe I do need a dollar. Or a shrink. Or a bag over my head. (Sticker smiles are the kind that look like they're slapped onto someone's face because the person doesn't really want to smile but doesn't know what else to do. I've been getting *lots* of these since December.) People don't know what to do with me, even though I'm pretty much the same as I always was. Too skinny, pretty smart, too serious according to Murphy, and good with words according to Dad.

■ ■ ■

Here was my after-school routine: Run up the twelve steps to the apartment while counting them. Unlock the door, walk inside, and soak in the sunlight. If the sun's out, the light at 3:35 p.m. is perfect, no matter what season (pink in winter, white in spring, yellow in fall). Plus, you can see the sunlight easier when it's quiet, and at 3:35 p.m., there was no one home except Axl Rose, Dad, and me. The three quietest beings that lived at 305 Water Street, Apartment B.

Then I'd drink Kool-Aid and eat Doritos and watch *Scooby-Doo* until four p.m. Then I'd sit at the kitchen table and do my homework. I'd hear the shower come on and know Dad was awake. He'd come out in his blue uniform with his hair slicked and combed, even though he didn't leave for work for six more hours.

I asked Murphy about this, when we were at the funeral home the first time. Picking out hymns and Bible verses and all that. Which was really Mom's call because Dad didn't believe in God. That I know of. "Why'd he get dressed for the graveyard shift so early?" I asked, and Murphy shook his head.

"I don't know. I think he was proud he could keep a job, and he wanted us to see him that way. Considering some guys he knew." He shrugged. "They couldn't do crap."

So Dad would sit down across from me in his uniform and pour a Jack Daniel's and sip on it while he read the newspaper. I don't know if it was a lot of liquor. The police asked me that. How much he drank. The glass was never very full and he sipped it very slowly. Like how an IV works in the hospital, I think. I told the police that too. He sipped it very slowly but he *did* need it. Once he forgot the bottle on a drive up north and we were deep in the woods and he started shaking like we were driving on gravel even though the road was just paved. Finally we found a gas station and he was okay. I didn't tell the police that part.

When I finished my homework, Dad would set up the Scrabble board and we'd play until Mom came home and made dinner. Sometimes he won and sometimes I did. I loved that. How evenly matched we were. How fair it was. He never let me win. And he never played BS words like "aa" that are technically words but are stupid to play on a Scrabble board. (The word "aa" according to the Oxford dictionary: basaltic lava forming very rough, jagged masses with a light frothy texture. The word "aa" according to me and Dad: bogus.)

Mom would talk and talk while she cooked, like someone had just let a parakeet into the apartment. Sometimes she would say, "Are you two even listening to me?" and I wasn't, but Dad always was. He would repeat a word back to her, and she'd nod, satisfied, and go on about Tiffany's deadbeat boyfriend or Tom's show-off attitude. Sometimes she would say, "What's the word I'm looking for?" and Dad would have it. Every time. " 'Pretentious,' " he'd say. Or "buoyant" or "unjust." Whatever he said, Mom would say, "Exactly." I loved that about him. How he would use most of his words on Mom. Mostly to make her feel heard.

I start to cry—inside the apartment that's sunny as ever, like making fun of me. What's the word? Mocking. Here's my routine now: Do my homework right away, on my bed, with the door closed. Drink Sprite. Watch anything but *Scooby-Doo*. Listen to 101.3 as loud as possible if I need to drown out my thoughts. Do nothing that reminds me of Dad.

■ ■ ■

Here's something weird: fried chicken smells amazing at any time of day. You don't even have to be hungry. You could have just been sleeping, like me right now. Murphy's sitting on the couch in his red KFC shirt with a bucket next to him, watching the North Stars. I can see the dent on his sweaty head where his visor was. He still has his nametag on. And his black shoes. He picks up his drink from the floor and sucks it through the straw and sets it back down without taking his eyes off the screen. Here's another weird thing: how much you love someone can sneak up on you in greasy moments that smell like fried chicken.

"Hey," I say, and plop down on the couch, next to the bucket.

"Hey, Monk. Want a drumstick? I got two for you."

"Yeah. Thanks." I find one and bite into it. Mom's not happy about Murphy working so many hours during high school, but I am. First of all, we need the money, and second of all, I get to eat KFC and watch hockey with my brother on a regular basis. If Murphy wasn't so beat from work, he'd be out with his friends like before. Which I guess is where he should be.

"Come *on*!" Murphy tells the North Stars.

"Who're they playing?" I should just watch and figure it out, but Murphy doesn't care that I know nothing about sports even though he knows everything.

"Toronto."

"Are we gonna win?"

"Well. We've won seventeen games and lost thirty-one so far. You're the brains of the family. What's our chances?"

"Not great."

Murphy laughs. "I'm gonna write that on my next math test and see what happens." I make Murphy's laugh repeat in my head so it lasts longer. I took it for granted before. It was always there, so I thought it always would be. Like Mom's parakeet dinner-making chatter. The two of them have gotten so quiet. Now Axl Rose meows all the time, and I blab on about nothing. Just to fill the space.

"Do you think people in Kentucky eat Kentucky Fried Chicken?" I ask.

"Prob'ly. They invented it."

"But do you think they like it, or do you think it's, like, chicken for Yankees and they eat better chicken?"

"I don't know, Monk. It's pretty good. *For that?*" Murphy yells at the TV. "You gotta be kidding me! They practically knocked Gagner unconscious! Is anyone wearing black-and-white stripes watching this game?"

The announcers mutter, agreeing with Murphy. A North Star glides into the penalty box and the door slams shut in front of him. He throws his stick down. They put up two minutes in lights. I hate the penalty box. It reminds me of how everyone looked at us after Dad died. We couldn't escape. We just had to sit there with the cameras on us. On our apartment window. On Mom's work. On Dad's work. On downtown Wicapi. On the train tracks. We just had to sit and wait for our time to run out. For something else to be more interesting.

Then Murphy's half walking, half carrying me to bed. I lie down and look up at him. "Who won?" I ask.

"We did. The good guys."

. . .

"Every seventh grader dissects a frog," Mr. Bauer tells us. "No ifs, ands, or buts. No religious excuses. I don't care if you're squeamish. This is what we do in seventh grade. And if you don't like it, go outside and wait for the purple bus." Mr. Bauer is always telling us to go outside and wait for the purple bus, which doesn't exist. As far as we know. Mr. Bauer is a grown man who wears unicorn suspenders and founded Wicapi's UFO club, so the purple bus might be real to him. Hard to say. "So today, to get you ready, we're doing sheep eyes."

This is no surprise because it's last period and the kids who already did sheep eyes have been bouncing the lenses like Super Balls in the hall all day. But some of the girls still cover their mouths like they might puke, and two boys pound their fists on the table like waiting for a meal, which is disturbing. "You want me to get it?" Kelly asks, and I nod. She slips down from the high stool, then carries the eye back carefully on its tray and sets it on the table between us. We look down at the eye, and it stares up at us. It's a brilliant, perfect sailing-on-Lake-Minnetonka blue.

"I—I'll be right back," I say, and bolt out of class. I can feel the stares behind me, and I hear Mr. Bauer say, "Don't worry about him. He'll catch the purple bus." I run through the empty hall and down the ramp, past the mural we did with the visiting artist last year. We all got to paint a tile, and when we put them together, it was one big picture of sailboats on the lake. I chose a solid blue one. I didn't want to screw anything up.

I push out the front doors and throw up on a snowbank.

"Great," I say to the puke. I wipe my mouth on my sleeve and turn both hands into fists, but there's no one to fight but me. I kick the snowbank, and it's ice and hurts my toe through my shoe. I was just starting to be invisible again. After six weeks of being *that kid,* seeing our family picture from the church directory on TV (Mom made Dad go on picture Sunday), and hearing the whispers in the stores, always the same words: "trolley . . . drunk . . . Vietnam . . . What did you expect?" I wanted to scream, *You don't know what you're talking about! You didn't even know him!* It was just starting to fade, at the edges. But I had to do something *so stupid* like puking from a sheep eye to bring it back.

Mom taught me whenever I feel out of control to just be quiet and listen. Something about sound grounding your body. She used to do it with Dad, back before us. When he had more problems. So I try it. I hear the wind. The flag flapping on the pole. A bird in a tree, tossing its voice up and down like the branch it's bobbing on. Then the grind of a school bus, turning in the long driveway. I listen to it chug closer. It pulls up right next to me. Number 243. It's my bus. Rodney pulls the handle, and the door smacks open.

"Hey, little man!" He takes off his neon-green sunglasses. "What are you doing out here? It's like, thirteen degrees!" I shrug. "Get in here!"

I climb the steps and sit in the front seat. The bus is warm and smells weird, but not bad weird, maybe like cinnamon. A dramatic song is blaring on the radio. Rodney takes a sip from a big thermos. He's wearing his jean jacket and his shirt half unbuttoned, and about five cross necklaces. Some kids asked him last week if he was cold, but he said he's committed to fashion. "Want some tea?" he asks. I shake my head. "You like this song?"

"I'm kind of sick of it."

"Yeah. She can sing, though. You're more into rap?"

"Not really. I like Metallica."

Rodney nods, and his one dangly silver earring swings. "A metalhead. I dig. So, what're you doing outside with no coat and no backpack? You didn't get kicked out, did you? Stay in school, man!" He points his thermos at me. "Do whatever you can! I got kicked out one too many times, and look at me."

"But you're the coolest bus driver. Everyone thinks so."

"They do? That's so rad. But still. Stay in school. You're a smart kid, I can tell. What's your name?"

"Justin."

"Yeah, Justin. You could be a lawyer with that name. Or a doctor. You wanna be a doctor?"

"No. I just threw up looking at a sheep eye."

"Oh man. You got Bauer?"

"Yeah."

"He still talkin' about that purple bus?"

I laugh. "Yeah."

"Those sheep eyes are foul. I don't blame you."

I shake my head. "I wasn't grossed out by the eye. It's just . . . This is gonna sound weird."

Rodney sets his thermos down. "I love weird!"

"It was just . . . seeing something dead. It reminded me of my dad. He died. So . . ."

Rodney clamps his huge hand on my shoulder. "That's heavy, dude. I'm sorry."

"Thanks."

"I never knew my dad," Rodney says.

"Really?"

"Nope. Never did. Wish I had, though. Some things I'd like to ask him. Did you know yours?"

I nod. "Yeah. Mostly I did."

"Well, that's a blessing."

. . .

From outside, where the wind's blowing so hard it's rattling our loose window, this looks like the perfect scene. Just Phuc and me playing Mario and eating microwave popcorn for lunch. Except the game keeps freezing and I can't stop thinking about how I should fix that window, to help out, but I have no idea how. Should I just stick some cardboard in it? Fold up a cereal box?

The game freezes (again).

"Try blowing in it," Phuc says. I take the game out (again) and blow in it (again). Then I blow in the Nintendo (again), pop the game back in, and turn it on. Mario runs across the screen. "Yeah!" Phuc says, shaking his controller. "We're back!"

I sit back down on the couch. "Dude. Sorry my Nintendo's so crappy. It's super old."

"No worries."

"And sorry I only have one game. Maybe we should go to your house."

"No way. I love it here. It's so peaceful." Phuc has three little sisters, but they're so loud it feels more like seven. "No one's begging me to play My Little Pony. No one's trying to brush my hair with a Barbie brush. No one's shrieking for no apparent reason. You got it made." Phuc looks over at me. "I mean—I didn't mean you got it made, like . . ."

I shake my head. "No, it's cool. I get it." We keep playing, up through the worlds. "Sometimes it's like, too quiet though," I tell Phuc.

"Yeah. Where is everyone?"

"Murphy's at work and Mom's at church."

"On Saturday?"

"Yeah, she's at church a lot now. When she's not working. She's on some committee. Then she does a ministry. I forget the name of it." Mario takes the vine up above the smiley clouds. My favorite part. It makes me feel like I'm on a different planet, which, if your dad gets killed in a ridiculous way in front of a crapload of people and it's all over the news, is a pretty awesome way to feel. "Then Sundays, obviously."

"Huh. I didn't know she was that religious."

"She's not. Or she wasn't before. I don't know."

Phuc shrugs. "There's worse things. Like barfing when you see a sheep eye."

"Shut up. How'd you hear about that?"

"Dude. Everyone heard about that."

"Great."

"No one cared, though. I mean like, it wasn't a big deal. All the girls were like, 'Poor Justin. He's been through so much, and now he had to see a sheep eye. Boo-hoo.' "

I pause the game, pick up a couch pillow, and smack him as hard as I can. He smacks me back. We get into a war, and it feels good to hit and throw and sweat and yell and run. Maybe I should take up boxing. I need some kind of hobby, because sitting in the apartment by myself all the time is making me crazy. And when I say "crazy" I mean it. Yesterday I had a whole conversation with Axl Rose (I had to do her part, since she's a cat) just to break the quiet.

■ ■ ■

"Mr. Olson!" the nurse calls when she walks me into Grandpa's room. I walked all the way here, which was far and cold, but it's better than being home alone all day while Murphy fries chicken and Mom switches church from Epiphany to Lent. Even if it does smell like spinach and medicine and the lady who sits by the front door always tries to hold my hand.

"You have a Sunday visitor!" the nurse says, and turns Grandpa's wheelchair from the window toward me. He smiles sweetly while the birds he was watching keep flitting around behind his head like a Disney movie. His bed is perfectly made with a tan blanket and flannel pillowcase and a throw pillow featuring a wood duck. Maybe they're trying to convince him he's up north at the cabin instead of in a nursing home. We told him about Dad, obviously, but we didn't know if he understood, so we told him a bunch more times. Then we stopped telling him because it just seemed mean.

"Hi, Grandpa," I say. "I'm your grandson, Justin. Larry's son." He nods politely. He lifts his hand up from his lap, then sets it back down. He shrugs a little. "Grandpa, can I look at your pictures? The old ones of Dad? In the book?" He blinks at me, which I decide means yes. I pull the photo album out of the top drawer, where it sits next to a row of socks under a sticker that says SOCKS, which seems unnecessary. I sit on Grandpa's bed with the book on my lap. Dad labeled all the people for Grandpa when his mind started to wander off. I slide my finger across Dad's handwriting, blocky and wide, and realize he'll never write anything again. A grocery list. A birthday card. A letter to me at college.

And Dad was always writing because he couldn't keep thoughts in his head very long. He'd walk into a room and forget why he was there. He'd set alarms but couldn't remember what to do when they went off. Once, he came home from the grocery store so mad because he couldn't remember one single thing he was supposed to get. So Mom went to the paper shop and got this really expensive stationery with his initials on it, in curly writing, like a wedding invitation. And guess what? It worked. He used up the whole pack in a week. But how did Mom know to do that?

I wipe my tears off with the back of my hand and start reading the names to Grandpa. He smiles, hearing them. I get to Dad's birth, and narrate his life out loud. "There's Larry as a baby. There he is at school. There he is playing hockey. He played defense, right, Grandpa?" Grandpa nods. "High school graduation. There he is in his uniform." I stare at Dad, smiling, clean-cut, ready. I turn the page, and he's with Mom, holding baby Murphy. Dad's hair is longer. He's got a mustache. He's still smiling, but his eyes are different. I flip the page back and forth, back and forth. Grandpa watches me. There's only a couple years missing between them, but I guess that space holds a lot.

I keep going. Murphy on a tricycle. Murphy holding me up like a trophy with my head flopped back. Murphy playing T-ball. Me in a baby swing. Me going to kindergarten. Murphy and me at the beach. "Look, Grandpa! Look at you and that walleye!" I turn the book around to show him. He's standing tall and straight like a pine tree next to Dad, holding a yellow-spotted fish with both hands. The fish is probably two feet long and its top fin is spiked up like a punk rocker. But Grandpa looks away, like either the dying fish or the dead son is too painful.

I turn the book back around and see a picture I never noticed before, of just Mom and Dad. It's a little blurry, and the colors are faded. They're watching something. Mom is maybe calling out to someone. Dad is smiling. And in the very far bottom left corner, they're holding hands. In one way, the words are true: "trolley . . . drunk . . . Vietnam . . . What did you expect?" And in another way, they're not.

CHAPTER TWO

"This is so bogus," I tell Murphy. "Why can't Mom get the groceries? It's nine-thirty on a school night. We're gonna look like orphans."

Murphy laughs and slams his car door, then kicks it, which is the only way to get it to shut all the way. "It's not a big deal," he says. "It's just the basics." We walk toward the lit-up store, even though I'd rather stay in the dark parking lot, like a little criminal. "You ever heard of Maslow's hierarchy of needs?" Murphy asks.

"No, but I bet my social worker would be into it. You should ask her."

"Ha. We learned it in psychology class." Murphy is bonkers about his psychology class. We walk through the automatic doors, and Murphy jerks a cart free from the line. It clangs and a woman looks over at us. I give her a sticker smile.

"It's a triangle," Murphy tells me. "At the bottom is your basic needs, right? Food and water. Shelter. Then it goes up from there." He pushes the cart toward the dairy section, where a cow smiles down at us from the brown wall. I bet they don't smile in real life, though. I bet they kick.

"Then safety's the next level, then love and belonging," Murphy says. He actually says "love and belonging" out loud like that. In his regular voice. Then he starts jogging, getting up speed, and *rides the cart*! I walk fast to catch up, but Murphy stops in front of the yogurt. "Then it's self-esteem, then self-actualization at the top," he tells me.

"What's the point?"

"The point is, you have to get your basic needs met before you can think about smart stuff like philosophy and physics and whatever else is in your head." He taps my forehead. "Bread comes first."

"What's 'self-actualization'?"

"Achieving your full potential. That's why it's a triangle. 'Cause all the masses are stuck at the bottom, trying to get their basic needs met. Not that many make it to the top, like you."

"I'm not at the top." I think of Mitchell poking me in the ribs and calling me a loser. Probably I'm at safety.

But Murphy smiles. "Yes you are. You're our monk on a mountaintop."

We keep walking. No one's around, but I keep my voice low anyway. "Murph? I'm sorry you have to do this. I'm sorry you're grocery shopping with me instead of out with your friends. And I'm sorry you have to work at KFC."

Murphy smiles. "I like hanging out with you." He turns the cart into the cereal aisle.

"That's not what I meant. Can I get Lucky Charms?"

"Sure." I get the biggest box because Murphy won't notice. In fact, he's watching all the cereal boxes roll by, in a blurred rainbow. "It's different now anyway," he says. "Most of my friends don't . . ." He shakes his head like trying to chase away whatever thought's trying to land in it.

Then he speeds the cart up again and takes the corner on two wheels.

...

The only good thing about the girls in pink and red sweaters arriving to pass out the heart-o-grams is that we have sixty seconds less of geography. I know I won't get any heart-o-grams, so I keep searching for Mali in my book so I can write it on the worksheet. It's insane. Why can't we just study out of the book? And then, after we write all the countries on the worksheet, we have to color them in with colored pencils. Like we're in third grade.

"Justin," a pink girl says, and drops three heart-o-grams onto my open book. They cover all of sub-Saharan Africa.

Three? Oh man. Did my mom hear about heart-o-grams somehow and send them? It's too embarrassing. My stomach's flipping around, which makes it even more embarrassing, because why do I even care? I open the first one. It's in Phuc's serial-killer handwriting and says, *What's up, loser? Your friend, Phuc.* I smile. The next one is in perfect cursive and says, *Hi, Justin. We miss you at book club. Hope you'll join us soon! Mrs. Peterson.* I miss book club too. But going back would violate my very strict rule of doing nothing that reminds me of Dad, who checked out all the book club books at the library and read them at the same time as me. So, nothing I can do. The third heart-o-gram is not from my mom. It says: *Hey, Justin. Happy Valentine's Day! Love, Jenni.*

. . .

When Mom gets home from work, I'm sitting alone at the kitchen table with only the oven light on, and I'm staring at the pizza that has three minutes left. My stomach's growling and I'm thinking about how after the pizza comes out, I still have to wait for it to cool. I should've started sooner. I didn't think the oven would take so long to preheat.

Mom gets confused and thinks I'm sad and starts fluttering around like she does when I'm sick, turning lights on and back off and asking if she can get me anything and am I thirsty and how was my day and did anything happen?

"Do you need to talk?" she asks. "Did something happen?"

"You already asked me that," I tell her.

"What?"

"If something happened. You asked me twice."

She sits down and reaches her hand across the table, then inches it back, like remembering that twelve-year-old boys don't hold their moms' hands anymore. "Well, did it?"

"No. Mom, I'm just hungry. Chill."

"I'm sorry. I shouldn't work late. You're on your own too much. It's not right."

"I like being on my own," I lie.

"Still."

"And we need the overtime." The oven buzzes. *Finally.* I start to get up, but Mom beats me to it and I let her.

"Where'd you hear that?" she asks.

I roll my eyes. "I live here. In the bedroom at the end of the hall? With Murphy?" She mom-glares at me, which looks like a real glare but isn't. "Have some pizza," I tell her. "Or at least give me some before I starve to death."

"Okay." She dishes the pizza out onto paper plates and pours Mr. Pibb into two cups. I blow so hard on my slice that I spit on it, then eat it too soon and burn the roof of my mouth.

"I do have a situation, though," I tell Mom when

my stomach fills up enough that I can think straight. She raises her eyebrows. She's trying to be cool so I won't scare off. Like when Grandpa tried to teach me to clean fish. "We have these stupid things at school. They're called heart-o-grams. So a girl sent me one, but I didn't send her one because I didn't know she was sending me one." Mom nods, slowly, like I just gave her instructions for saving an entire planet and all of its living creatures. I laugh.

"What? I'm listening!"

I laugh some more. "I know. It's just, it's not that serious. Anyway, I don't want her to think I don't like her. I mean, I don't like her like her, like that. I just like her like she's a nice person. But I can't send her a heart-o-gram now 'cause Valentine's Day is over. So what should I do?" This is a lie. I do like her like her. But I didn't realize it until now so I'm not counting it as a lie. Plus it's my mom, so even if I knew it was a lie, I might have still said it. No way to know.

Mom squints, like she's trying to see the answer in the distance. I squint back at her.

"Knock it off," she says. "Okay. Why don't you just write her a note and stick it in her locker?"

"And say what?"

"I don't know. 'Thanks for the heart-o-gram. Sorry I didn't send you one, but I forgot my money. It was really nice, though. Happy Valentine's Day.'"

I smile. "Pretty good, Mom."

She shrugs. "Thanks."

Then it hits me. It's Valentine's Day. And Mom. And Dad. And maybe she was the sad one and I didn't notice because I was so freaking hungry. "Happy Valentine's Day, Mom!" I blurt out.

"Thanks."

"Sorry I didn't get you anything."

She laughs. "No problem. That's not your job."

"This is a really crappy Valentine's. Sorry."

"No, it's not. And don't say 'crappy.'"

"Okay."

"Seriously, Justin? All that stuff is overrated. I'm totally content with you, a frozen pizza, and Mr. Pibb."

"Yeah. He's such a romantic."

■ ■ ■

"Mr. Engstrom. Your own country is at war. Don't you want to understand why?" Mr. Sorenson insists on calling us by our last names like we're adults, even though we're very obviously not. He looks like a college professor instead of a junior high history teacher. He's got a white beard that he keeps perfectly trimmed and he wears spectacles and tweed jackets with elbow patches. I don't know if there's a technical difference between glasses and spectacles, but his are definitely spectacles. If they let teachers smoke in here, I know he'd have a pipe. He's super smart. I don't know why he's wasting his time on us.

"I know why," Brandon replies.

"Care to enlighten us?"

"'Cause Saddam Hussein's *in*sane, and we need to take him out."

The class murmurs and laughs. "Not a very precise analysis, Mr. Engstrom," Mr. Sorenson says. But Brandon doesn't hear him. He's turned back around, sliding his finger across Josh's desk to show how some hockey play went last night. A finger from his left hand slams the one from his right, and Josh pumps his fist in the air. They high-five.

Mr. Sorenson clears his throat. "We tend to think of history as inevitable," he says. "But look at what just happened. Congress voted to use military force in Iraq, fifty-two to forty-seven in the Senate, and two hundred fifty to one hundred eighty-three in the House." He writes the numbers on the board, trying to make them mean more to us. "Those are the closest margins in authorizing military force since the War of 1812." He looks at me. "Things can always go a different way."

I copy Mr. Sorenson's map from the board, with the arrows showing advancement and the circles for bombs. Dad was a news junkie. He read three newspapers a day and ran news radio like it was oxygen. He watched the war ramp up all last fall. The planes, the troops arriving in Saudi Arabia, it was all on TV. It didn't feel real. It felt more like a video game. But Dad knew better. He'd pace, especially when they showed the troops close-up. They didn't look much older than Murphy. Two hundred thousand troops. Then one hundred thousand more a few weeks later, like they'd miscalculated somehow. After Thanksgiving the UN gave Saddam until January fifteenth to get out of Kuwait. "You think he will, Dad?" I asked. "You think he'll leave?" Dad shook his head and left the room.

But before he left for work that night, he came

into my room. "Son," he said, and I bolted straight up, like lightning struck my bed. Dad didn't spend many words on me. Especially big ones like "son."

"Don't become a soldier," he said. And I said, "Yes, sir," even though I never called him "sir." He walked to the doorway and the hall light crossed his body, making half of him shine.

"Nothing is as simple as it seems," he said. I nodded. "Good night." He shut the door and I counted the words. Fourteen. All for me.

Dad was right, even though he didn't live to see it. Saddam didn't leave Kuwait, and we "bombed the piss out of them," as Brandon would say, on January seventeenth. I hadn't gone back to school yet, so I watched it all day on CNN. When Mom came home and shut the TV off, I couldn't really see her, my eyes were so dry and blurry. "Okay. That's enough horror for one day," she said. "Get your coat. We're going to the Platter." And I wondered, *Is that how she handled Dad? How she pulled him through?* Just, *That's enough, let's get some pizza?* Anyway, after all those bombs, the war's still going. Ground troops mostly. It's going well, I guess. No one's really watching.

. . .

I'm on my way to the office to get more paper for
Mrs. Peterson because she prints five million poems
a day, and I'm taking my time because the halls are
peaceful when they're empty. I'm trying to think of
other peaceful/empty things (the Grand Canyon, new
notebooks) when I realize Jenni is walking toward
me. Time gets gooey, like a Jolly Rancher left in a hot
car. We're moving so slow, and then suddenly she's
right in front of me. She smells like oranges even
though it's the dead of winter, which reminds me of
Mrs. Peterson telling us how Laura Ingalls Wilder
was *thrilled* to get an orange in her Christmas stock-
ing. Which would totally suck.

"Hey," Jenni says.

"Hey."

"Thanks for the note."

"Oh. Yeah. Sorry I didn't send you a heart-o-gram.
I just . . ."

She shakes her head. "It's totally fine. Those things
are kind of crazy anyways."

"Yeah."

"Are you ever coming back to book club?"

"I don't know." I shove my hands in my pockets. We're standing in the main entry, which is all glass and flooded with white winter light. Jenni's hair is full of static, like maybe she just took her hat off, and the tiny blond strands hover in the air.

"We're reading *Fahrenheit 451*. It's a tenth-grade book, but Peterson says we can handle it. It's futuristic. You'd like it, I think. It's about real things."

I nod. "Sounds cool."

"Yeah. Well, I gotta get back to band. See ya."

"See ya."

She walks away, but my body's stuck like it refuses to leave this moment, with the sparkly light and the girl who likes real things. "Hey!" I call to Jenni. "What instrument do you play?"

She keeps walking but turns her head and calls back, "Tuba!"

I give her a thumbs-up, and she laughs. Then she's gone, around the corner. I take a deep breath and whisper to the empty space, "That girl is so cool."

. . .

As much as I didn't want to come to Prince of Peace Lutheran Church on a Wednesday, it actually feels pretty good to sit in the same red cushion pews and see the same old ladies way up front and hear the babies crying in the back. We stand up to sing the first song, and Murphy slides in next to me, smelling like chicken and cologne. I cough and wave a hand in front of my face.

"Shut up," he whispers. "Hi, Mom!" She beams at him and manages to sing, pick up another hymnal, turn it to the right page, and hand it to Murphy, without missing a word. Moms are kind of amazing that way.

"Why are we at POP on a Wednesday?" Murphy asks me. "I had to take a double on Saturday to be off tonight."

I shrug. "They're trying something new. Lenten Soup and Service. Mom's into it."

"Is it always Lenten soup? What's wrong with chicken noodle?"

"You're such an idiot."

It turns out that the service part of Lenten Soup and Service is super short, so pretty soon we have our soup (ham and wild rice—shocker) and rolls and pop and fake Oreos, and we're sitting at the end of a long table in the church basement.

"So," Mom says. "What are you two giving up for Lent this year?"

Murphy swallows half his roll in one gulp. "I'm gonna give up punching Justin." He slugs me in the shoulder. "Oh well. Better luck next year."

"I'm going to give up Lenten soup," I say. "Oh, that was easy. 'Cause it doesn't exist."

Mom rolls her eyes, but I can tell she's happy because it's the first time we've been kind of ourselves in a long time. *What did you expect?* is still floating around the church basement, but I block it out. They didn't know him. He never came here, except on picture day. But Mom's been spending so much time at church that all kinds of people stop at our table to say hi.

"Mom," Murphy says after a while, "you're like the queen of POP." Then he grins and nods at us because he made a pretty decent joke by accident.

"Murphy!" A gray-haired man wearing khaki pants and a royal-blue Minnetonka sweater walks up.

Murphy turns, wipes his right hand on his pants, and holds it out for the guy to shake. "Hey, Coach."

"How are you, son?"

"Fine, sir. You know my mom. And this is my little brother, Justin."

Coach smiles at us. "Hey, everybody. Nice to see you. Listen, Murphy. We really missed you at tryouts." He puts a hand on the back of Murphy's chair and leans down. "What's going on?"

Mom's whole face falls and goes pale. Murphy looks down, then back up at Coach. "I've been workin' a lot, Coach."

Coach nods. "I see." His eyes are sad, like Mom's. I can tell because his glasses make them humungous. He straightens back up. "Well, you just call me if you change your mind. Practice starts in a couple weeks, and you've *always* got a spot on my team."

"Thanks, Coach. I will."

"Murphy," Mom whispers after he walks away. "Why didn't you go out for baseball?"

Murphy stirs his soup around. "It's not a big deal, Mom. Hockey's really my sport. Baseball I just do for fun. Plus the hockey coaches are always worried I'll throw my arm out, so I'm just . . . taking the season off." He looks up, finally. "Maybe I'll play senior year."

Mom leans forward. "We don't need money so bad

that you can't play baseball, Murph." She's still whispering, like she's afraid of what her voice might do if she lets it get louder. "You're seventeen. You're supposed to just do things for fun."

"Yeah, dude." I pat him on the back. "You got your whole life to work at KFC."

Mom frowns at me. "Please play, Murphy," she says.

"Yeah, please play," I tell him. "I like the peanuts."

But Murphy looks away. "I'll think about it."

■ ■ ■

Another frozen Saturday. I start walking without a plan because I can't sit alone in the apartment for one more second. The sun is shining in a surprisingly blue sky. I try not to think about the sheep eye. And the sheep it belonged to. I walk down by the beach covered in snow and circle back up the hill. Then past the end of Water Street and the corner bar and the expensive apartments facing the lake and the paper shop. And guess where I end up? The train tracks. The exact spot where Dad got killed, and before I can stop myself, I look for blood. There isn't any, obviously, 'cause it's been washed away by a hundred snowfalls. Or maybe he only bled on the inside.

They wouldn't let me see him at the hospital. I found out later it was because he was already dead. The doctor came to the waiting room to explain it to us. Mom was holding Murphy's hand and I was sitting on the floor but I don't know why. There were plenty of chairs. "The trolley wasn't moving that fast," the doctor said. "It's just the way he fell, and the place on his head that hit the tracks. It hit in just the right spot."

"You mean just the wrong spot?" I asked, and the doctor looked down at me. He was so young! Couldn't they get anyone better than this guy? He still had baby cheeks! He should have been flipping burgers at Arnold's, not saving lives (or not) in the ER.

His baby cheeks turned pink. "Sorry," he said. "Yes, the wrong spot. It hit in the wrong spot." Then my memory blurs for a while. That night comes in and out. The next thing I remember is Pastor Steve with an expression I'd never seen before and hope I never see again. What's the word? Grim. He's always so smiley at church. He has a cup full of candy on his desk and lets us take as much as we want. He just keeps refilling it. Isn't that awesome? Every grown-up in the history of the world with a cup of candy has a rule about how many pieces you can take. But not Pastor Steve.

There's a bench at the train tracks so I sit on it, even though the snow will soak through my pants and freeze me. It's a totally normal place, to anyone else. Just the track coming in and the circle where the trolley turns around. The lake is frozen and white with its ice house city on top. Dad took me ice fishing a few times, when his buddy let him borrow his house. It was strangely warm in that house on the ice. Dad and I got so hot we took our jackets off. I start laughing at that, like a crazy person, but stop before I say "Remember, Dad?" out loud. Because that would be just too much. But is that what crazy people are? Just people talking to the dead?

. . .

When Brandon and his buddies walk in and see the TV at the front of the room, they all yell "Movie day!" which is idiotic because Mr. Sorenson never shows movies. There's only one word on the board: CEASE-FIRE.

"Never heard of that one," Brandon says as he slides into his desk next to mine. "You?" I just stare at him, so he asks again, slower, like I'm stupid. "Olson. You . . . ever . . . heard . . . of the movie . . . *Cease-Fire*?"

"It's . . . It's not a movie. It's a thing," I tell him. "That happened."

Brandon drops his chin toward his chest and widens his eyes, like the parrot in the art room. He says, "Okay. Well, good talkin' to ya, Olson."

Mr. Sorenson turns off the lights, and the blue glare from the TV makes us instantly quiet. President Bush comes on the screen, sitting at his desk in the Oval Office. Mr. Sorenson turns the volume up. "Kuwait is liberated," the president says. "Iraq's army is defeated." The class cheers.

Brandon reaches over and slaps me on the back. "Cease-fire!" he yells.

"Kuwait is once more in the hands of Kuwaitis, in control of their own destiny," the president says. His voice fills the dark room, all the way to the walls.

This is a time of pride, he tells us. Our victory was quick, decisive, and just. It was a victory for all mankind, for the rule of law, for what is right. But I can hear Dad's voice too, small, in a corner of my head. *Don't become a soldier,* he says. "We can be a catalyst for peace," the president says. "This war is now behind us." Dad says, *Nothing is as simple as it seems.*

"Let us give thanks to those who risked their lives," the president says. "Let us never forget those who gave their lives." Is he talking about Dad? I mean, I know he's talking about the soldiers who died in *this* war. But is Dad included, when people thank soldiers who gave their lives? Because in a way he did give his life. And in another way, he got drunk and got hit by a trolley. "May God bless our valiant military forces and their families, and let us all remember them in our prayers," says President Bush. Is that us? Mom and Murphy and me? Dad says, *Good night.*

CHAPTER THREE

Phuc stayed after school for math team so I'm sitting alone on the bus, watching tiny houses pass by with snow high in all the yards and curvy paths shoveled to the doorways. I picture walking up each path, living in that house or that one or that one. Would it be better? Or worse? We pass one that belongs to an old lady whose yard Mom made me rake once. The lady gave me one dollar. She was so grateful there were tears in her eyes. I tried to give the dollar back, but she wouldn't take it. I didn't want to spend it, so I just stuck it in my sock drawer. I see it sometimes and wonder about her, if she still needs help. If she's still alive. Weird that I don't just ask

Mom. Or walk up to her door and knock. Maybe I don't really want to know.

"Yo, little bro," Rodney says softly, like trying not to startle me. I look up and he smiles at me in the rearview mirror. The bus is empty and still. Mine's the last stop. I stand up and swing my backpack onto one shoulder and walk down the gritty, slushy aisle that Rodney will have to clean as the last thing. I imagine him singing as he slides his mop down the aisle, the sky dark and all the cars rushing home to their golden windows and dinners on the table. I wonder where Rodney goes. I hope he has a golden window.

"Deep in thought today," he says when I get to the front. He's wearing a Vikings hat with a yellow puffball on top that should seem out of place with his earring, but on Rodney, somehow everything works together.

I shrug. "I guess."

"Something on your mind?"

I should say, *Yes.* I should say, *Lots of things.* I should say, *Was my dad destined to die? Are the words mostly true? Trolley, drunk, Vietnam, what did you expect? Was it—what's the word? Inevitable?*

Was he a walking ghost? A ticking bomb? Were we just biding our time? And also, *Did he do it on purpose?* Rodney's a man. He could take it.

Instead I say, "Not really."

"Okay. Just know I'm here for you. I got eight whole minutes before basketball pickup."

"Thanks, Rodney." I go down the three sloshy steps, and I'm out in the cold.

Rodney calls down through the open door. "Hey, next time you see Bauer, tell *him* to get on the purple . . . Wait, no, don't tell him that." He pauses, then makes a fist and says, "Keep up the good fight!"

. . .

"Want a grilled cheese?" Murphy asks. He's standing at the stove holding a spatula.

"Yeah. Thanks." I look into the pot. "Tomato soup too? Chef Murphy."

Murphy smiles. "Yeah, right. All I can make is grilled cheese."

"Not true. Once you made toast."

"You got me."

"Why aren't you at work?"

"I actually only work six days a week. Can you believe it? It's my night off."

"And on the seventh day he made grilled cheese," I say. Murphy smiles and lays another piece of bread in the pan and it sizzles. "So are you gonna play baseball or what?"

He sighs. "Nope."

"Mom really wants you to. It would mean a lot to her."

"Yeah. I know."

"So why don't you?"

"Because, Justin. I can't just think like you and Mom. It's different now. I have to think like Dad. And Dad took care of his family first."

"Not really!" I yell, surprising both of us. "He got drunk and got hit by a Christmas trolley. Do you know how embarrassing that is?" Murphy blinks at me. "Have you ever gone to seventh grade after your dad got *killed by a Christmas trolley driving twenty miles an hour?*" Murphy waits. "Well I have, and it *sucks!*"

"He didn't mean for it to happen," Murphy says quietly.

"Maybe he did. Maybe he didn't. But it happened.

And if this family's in trouble, that's Dad's fault. Not yours. Just play baseball, Murphy!" I start to cry. I can't help it. Actually, maybe I can help it, but I don't try. "Please play baseball!"

Murphy turns his head and wipes a few tears away so I won't see them.

"Just *play*!" I sob. My chest starts to catch and heave like a car breaking down.

Murphy pulls me to him and bear hugs me. I want so bad to sit on the bleachers with Mom and watch Murphy play ball. I've never wanted anything more in my entire life, which makes me realize that Laura Ingalls Wilder possibly wasn't so lame for wanting an orange for Christmas. Life is crazy that way. Probably especially on the prairie.

"I wish I could, Monk," Murphy says. "Maybe next year, okay?" He pats my back. "Maybe next year."

■ ■ ■

I'm back on the bench at the place where Dad died, staring at the frozen lake. Before Grandpa stopped talking, all his conversations were about birds. He had a stack of bird books on his nightstand and Dad strung up like ten bird feeders on a wire outside his window at the nursing home so Grandpa could watch birds all day. Going to visit him was the worst, because what do you say about a nuthatch except "Yep. There he is." And what would I say about these ice houses in their little rows except "Yep. There they are."

"Hello," a voice says. I look up and stare. It's Benny H., the most famous man in Wicapi. Our only homeless man. I mean, technically he's not homeless. (They should put that on a bumper sticker. *Wicapi! A town where not even the homeless man is homeless!*) He has a bedroom at his sister's house, but Benny H. doesn't like to stay there. He likes the streets. And the library. He always sits at a table in the nonfiction section, where I only go if I have to do a report for school. I heard he used to be a history professor, but I guess something happened. The bakery gives him one cup of coffee and one doughnut for free every morning. I don't know if he has any other deals in town. I don't know why he wanders around either, but he's been doing it since way before I was born, so no one bothers to question it anymore. Benny H. just is Benny H.

"Hello," I say back.

"Mind if I sit?"

"No, I don't mind." I scoot over one centimeter, since I'm already at the end of the bench, but it seems like the polite thing to do. Benny H. sits down, and his body fills up most of the empty space. His winter beard's gotten long, and he's got his black top hat on. The edges of his ears are red, and his hands too. I've never been this close to him, except once in the library when I reached behind him to get a book on the snow leopard. He smells like smoke and leaves and baby powder. I look around to see if anyone's watching, but we're the only ones out. Which figures, since it's probably twenty degrees. "Um, Benny H.?" I ask.

"Yes."

"This isn't, like, your bench, is it? 'Cause I can move."

Benny H. laughs like a giant. I'm serious. Like the Jolly Green Giant statue on the way to Iowa might laugh if he wasn't, you know, a statue. Benny H.'s hair is matted and his coat is faded but that laugh comes from somewhere else. "No, these benches belong to the Town of Wicapi," he says. "They are equally yours and mine." I nod. I like the way he says "equally." "Not much to see with the ice on," he adds.

"I like to picture the fish swimming around underneath, doing everything they normally do. Like the ice doesn't even faze them." *Oh, jeez. Shut up, Justin!*

Benny H. turns and looks at me. His eyes are very green, like the algae in the lake in the summertime. "Is that so?" I shrug. "Did you know this lake was sacred to the Dakota?" He coughs for a few seconds, then pulls out a dark blue handkerchief and spits into it. "Used to be burial mounds all around here." He waves his hand at the lake. "Right where we're sitting."

"No way."

"True. Truth."

"What happened?" I ask.

"To the mounds?"

"Yeah."

"Well, we dug 'em up, of course. Got ourselves some souvenirs. Beads, pipes, bones. A real-life treasure hunt!" My stomach starts to feel like a slinky gathering speed down the stairs. "Then we plowed through 'em," Benny H. says. "Needed the farmland, ya know. Logged the trees. Needed those too. Built houses and roads and a whole town right on top of those holy bones. Laid down train tracks to Minneapolis. You go to school. You know the drill."

"Yeah." I go to school. But I'd never heard anything like this.

"You know Breezy Point?" Benny H. asks, and I nod. "That's where Spirit Knob used to be, right at the tip of a mound that reached sixty feet up." Benny H. looks up and so do I, like the mound might still be there, in spirit, in the sky. "It was the most sacred spot on the lake to the Dakota—where the lake got its power."

"What happened to it?" I ask, even though I don't want to know. At all.

"Leveled. In 1884. For a country club."

I look over at the hill sloping up by the baseball diamond, where we'd sit and watch Dad play softball when I was little. He was the right fielder, with the lake always tossing behind him. He had a strong arm. I can still picture him there, or his outline at least, like a ghost. And all around him I can see Dakota ghosts, ducking softballs while Dad's team warms up.

. . .

Of all the rooms in Minnetonka Junior High School, the cafeteria is the worst. The whisper words and sticker smiles and stares are everywhere. It's like the hallway times a billion. At least in the hallway you can keep moving. In the cafeteria you're just stuck. Like in the penalty box. Waiting for the bell to end it.

"Clam chowder day is the best," Phuc says, and rips open his pack of oyster crackers. Phuc, on the other hand, is perfectly happy in the cafeteria because Phuc is perfectly happy everywhere. He's like one of those catfish in Texas. When their pond dried up, they just evolved to grow feet and walked to the next pond. If I was a catfish and my pond dried up, I would definitely die.

"Are you serious?" I ask. "It's, like, literally the grossest soup ever."

"Nuh-uh," Phuc says. "Split pea is."

"You win."

"Anyway, I don't eat the soup. I'm working on my record."

"Oh. Right."

Phuc tosses up the crackers one by one and catches them in his open mouth. He misses on number seven. "Dang it!"

"What's your record again?" I ask.

"Eight. I'm gonna get all ten by the end of the year. Mark my words."

"You want my pack?"

"No. That's cheating." He looks down sadly at his clam chowder and puts his hands together like praying. "You have defeated me again, clam chowder. You are a worthy opponent." His mouth keeps moving after he stops talking, like the Japanese ninja movies he loves so much that are always out of sync. I smile. I can't help it. "So are you gonna ask Jenni-with-an-*i* to the dance?" he asks.

My stomach leaps into my chest, just hearing her name. How ridiculous. "Why would I?"

"She gave you a heart-o-gram. So. Your move." Phuc takes a bite of cheesy bread. It's the only thing you can eat on clam chowder day. Besides the crackers. And Phuc eats the tapioca pudding, but just the thought of those little balls makes me want to vomit.

"How do you know she gave me a heart-o-gram?"

Phuc swallows. "Dude, do you even listen when you walk through the halls?"

"No. When I walk through the halls, I do the opposite of listening." What I do: Pick a point, far away, and stare at it until I get there. Then pick another point. "Are you going to the dance?"

"No way," Phuc says. "There's a total lunar eclipse that night, and my mom just set up our new telescope."

"You're the biggest nerd alive."

"Thanks."

"Can I watch with you?"

"Sure, second-biggest nerd."

Mitchell walks by and bangs into my shoulder. "Sorry," he says. "Not."

We wait in silence while he walks away. Then I whisper to Phuc, "What's with that dude? He's been doing crap like that ever since I came back to school."

"You seriously don't know?"

"No. Do you?"

Phuc shakes his head like he can't imagine what it's like to be me, living under a rock. But it's more like living in a cloud. I see outlines of things, but it's hard to focus on them. "He likes Jenni-with-an-*i,* but she turned him down because, obviously, she likes you."

"Wait. How do you know this?"

"He gave her this super lame teddy bear for Christmas, and she, like, didn't want to take it and give him the wrong idea, I guess? I don't know. I heard it was super awkward."

"Great." I don't realize I'm staring at Mitchell until he catches my eye from over by the trash can, and smirks.

• • •

Mr. Bauer made the rookie mistake of setting packs of matches on all the tables and then leaving the room, so Mike is lighting matches one after another after another, letting each one burn until the very last second when the flame almost touches his thumb. Then a bunch of other kids start doing it too, and all the tiny fires all over the room remind me of my first day back at school after Dad died, the day the Iraqi army blew up the oil fields in Kuwait.

There were six hundred oil wells in flames, some burning black smoke and some white, so the whole scene was a bunch of fires spread out everywhere, and the ground in between them was black with orange in the cracks. It looked like the whole world was on fire.

It looked like a horror movie. Like the apocalypse. It was broad daylight, but the sun was a shadow behind the smoke. A soldier came on TV and said, "It looks like how I envision hell. The country of Kuwait is burning." I missed Dad so much at that moment I felt like I was burning too.

Then Mom switched the TV off and said, "Time to go."

"Where?"

"School."

"But it's a Tuesday," I told her. "Don't you think I should start on a Monday? Shouldn't you call first?"

Mom walked over to the couch, where I was staring at the empty TV screen but still seeing the choked-out sun, and put both hands on my shoulders. "Justin, sometimes you just gotta jump in. You know, like at the lake, how it's better to run off the end of the dock instead of sticking your toe in first?"

"The lake is not the same as seventh grade."

But I went. What choice did I have? And those fires stuck with me all week. I saw the halls and the kids and the classrooms and everything, but it was like there was smoke all around them, making everything hazy. And here's something even freakier:

they're still fighting those same fires. And they have no idea how long it will take. Yesterday on the news a reporter said there is "no timeline for completion." And I knew exactly what she meant.

. . .

When I first wake up, before real life comes back, I think Mom and Dad are in the kitchen because I hear the voices parents use when something's wrong but the kids are asleep. I walk out of my room, rubbing my eyes. The sun is a pale orange stripe behind the trees, and it's not Mom and Dad (obviously). It's Mom and Murphy. "Hey, Monk," Murphy says.

"Hey," I say. "What's wrong?"

"Car won't start. Go back to bed. It's early."

I sit down at the table. "No, I'm good. Can I help?"

Mom smiles. "Nothing to do. We're just figuring out how to get everyone where they need to go. You want some eggs?"

"No. I'll have cereal." Mom goes to the cabinet, but I get up. "I can get it," I tell her, and my voice comes out rougher than I mean it to.

She raises both hands, like surrendering. "Fine."

She and Murphy keep talking, about Mom's boss, who thinks he runs the world instead of a pharmacy, and Murphy's three tardies already this quarter, and maybe Mom can work late to make up for it. Maybe she can get a ride with Brenda. Maybe Jake can cover Murphy's shift tonight. Which tow truck was the one Jerry said was such a rip-off? I crunch my Frosted Flakes loud, trying not to listen.

They don't talk about the real problem, which is paying for the tow truck and whatever's wrong with the car. Because *One day at a time.* That's what Mom says now. When we had to pick the cheapest coffin, she said, *One day at a time.* When the hospital bill came, she said, *One day at a time.* When she slipped on the ice and wrapped her ankle in an Ace bandage and stood on it for the next eight hours counting pills and it swelled up like a water balloon, she said, *One day at a time.* When Murphy holds the phone to his chest and tells Mom it'll be eighty bucks to tow the car, I know what's coming. I run to my room and slam the door, just so I won't have to hear it.

. . .

Figures. Jenni's walking with five other girls. Five! Why do girls do that? Why are they never alone?

"Hi," she says, passing by.

"Hi." I lean against the wall and watch her keep walking. I'm never gonna talk to her. And why should I? She deserves someone better. Someone with clothes not from Kmart. Someone who knows the score of the North Stars game last night. Or who they played or if they even played at all. Someone who's not afraid of a school dance. But then her friends turn in to a classroom and she's still walking. Alone. I start running. Everyone's staring at me, but I've learned how to look straight ahead. She's getting closer and closer. She is my faraway point.

"Hey." I'm out of breath when I get to her.

"Hey. You okay?"

"Yeah. I just . . . I saw you, so I . . . ran."

"Yeah, I guess."

"Jenni."

"Yeah?" She stops walking and turns toward me, and her eyes get a little bigger.

"I can't ask you to the dance." Stupid, stupid.

"Okaaaay." Her cheeks turn a little pink, and she looks around to see who's listening.

"I'm sorry. I can't explain it. I just . . . can't." In my head, my fists are punching my brain. Kicking the crap out of it. She turns to go. *Do something! Anything!* "But, um. Do you like pizza?"

"I mean, I'm not an alien," she says.

"Huh?"

"Yes. I like pizza."

"Oh. Great. So, would you, like, want to go get some sometime? With me?"

She smiles and shrugs. "Sure."

"Thank you!"

Jenni laughs. "You know something, Justin? You're a unique person."

"Thanks?"

"You're welcome."

■ ■ ■

If there was a volume meter that measured houses, Phuc's would be a ninety-nine and mine would be a five. (Only because Axl Rose meows so much. Otherwise it would be a zero. Okay, maybe a one.) You would not believe how loud little sisters are. The good part is that Phuc has his own room. All three of his sisters have to share, and their room looks like a bottle of Pepto-Bismol exploded in the middle of it, then a bunch of ponies pranced in for a drink and puked up glitter. It's a nightmare. Phuc's room is small, but it has a glow-in-the-dark universe on the ceiling and NASA posters all over the walls and an iguana named Copernicus in a tank. Plus, Phuc's room is the only one that goes straight to the roof.

We climb out the window, and Phuc's dad already set out two lawn chairs with blankets in them, next to the telescope. Can you imagine? A dad setting out lawn chairs with blankets in them?

"Check it out," Phuc says. "It already started." The moon is massive and white and full in the cold sky, like the Georgia O'Keeffe painting in the art room, the one of a blooming white flower. A shadow is covering a sliver of one side.

"What's happening again?" I ask.

Phuc's bent down, looking through the telescope. "It's called a lunar eclipse," he says slowly.

"No duh, Phuc. You know what I mean."

"The earth is in between the sun and the moon, blocking the sunlight. So that shadow on the moon is earth's shadow." Truth: I can't really picture it. I try to make a textbook diagram in my head, but it doesn't work. "You look," Phuc says, and I do. In the telescope, the moon is more complicated than I realized.

For a long time, we stay quiet. Phuc only talks when he has something to say, which is the opposite of most people, who talk no matter what. Maybe it's 'cause of his sisters. He doesn't want to add any noise to the planet unless he has to. The shadow keeps moving across the moon, turning it more and more orange until the whole thing glows like a ball of red clay in the sky.

"Whoa," I say. "Why's it do that?"

"Only the red light can get through Earth's atmosphere," Phuc says. "All the other light scatters. So what you're actually seeing is all the planet's sunrises and sunsets reflected on the moon."

"No way."

"Way."

I picture all the people all over the world under all the sunrises and all the sunsets, just going about their lives and not knowing that everything is reflected on the moon. "So it's like everyone is . . . connected . . . on the moon," I say.

"Yeah. Kind of like superstrings."

Phuc's mom is a physicist at the U of M. "Phuc. Speak English."

"Superstrings are like, super, super small. We never see them. And the energy from their vibrations makes up the entire universe. All things."

"I thought atoms made up all things."

Phuc frowns at me. "Dude. No. So, because of superstrings, we have ten dimensions instead of four. Like, we can only see three dimensions of space and one of time, right?"

"Okay."

"But there are actually nine dimensions of space and one of time." His voice is revving up, like it might blast him off the roof and up into outer space to check it all out for himself. "And get this. The small dimensions are tucked into a bigger dimension, so we don't experience them. But the smaller dimensions are actually reality." He squints at me to make sure I'm paying attention. "Do you know what this means?"

He asked me the same question when they launched Hubble into space last year. Phuc claimed it was the most significant advance in astronomy since Galileo's telescope. Even when the first picture came back blurrier than his sister's Lite-Brite, he still believed. "Just wait," he'd said. "Give it time."

I laugh. "Of course I do. Not."

Phuc leans back in his chair and stares at the moon, fading back to white. "It means our whole reality is unreal." He shrugs and shakes his head. "It means the distinction between space and time is false. It means all times could be happening at the same time. Your past and your future could be happening all at once. Right now."

I shiver. Probably 'cause it's late and the temperature's dropping. But maybe because the idea of Dad getting hit by the Christmas trolley over and over in some other dimension makes me want to throw up.

CHAPTER FOUR

I wake up in the middle of the night and bolt up in my bed, like I did when Dad said my name in the dark, and here's why: If superstrings mean that all time is happening at the same time, does that mean Dad is alive in some other dimension? I dial Phuc's number before I can stop myself and his mom answers. "Hi, Mrs. Tran?"

"Justin? Are you okay?"

"Yeah. I just had a question for Phuc."

"It's after midnight. He's asleep. Could you ask him in the morning?" I picture the phone ringing in the Trans' silent house and the windows lighting up one by one like in that Christmas commercial, and all of Phuc's sisters jumping on their beds and never calming down again.

"Yeah. I'm sorry. I didn't mean to wake you."

But Mrs. Tran says, "You didn't."

"Oh. Mrs. Tran? Can I ask you the question instead? It's about the ten dimensions."

"I was just thinking about those myself. About black holes, actually, but it all connects." I try to imagine having a mom that sits and thinks about reality. I mean, actual reality and not the kind of reality that my mom sits and thinks about.

"Really?" I ask.

"Yes. We think so, anyway. What's your question?"

"Phuc said that all times are happening at once. So I was wondering. If the past is happening, does that mean people who are dead in the present are still alive somehow? In the past? In another dimension?"

There's silence on the phone, and my heart starts to beat in my eardrums. Maybe Phuc had it wrong. Maybe Dad is just dead. *Dead, dead, dead,* my heart says.

Mrs. Tran breathes in like she needs extra oxygen for the answer. "I can honestly say, Justin, I don't know. There's so much about space and time that we don't understand, that we don't perceive. We're discovering new things all the time. By the time you and Phuc are in college, I just can't imagine."

I smile, in the dark. The moon is tiny and white outside my window, like nothing amazing ever happened to it. Like it was never a blazing ball in the sky reflecting all the sunrises and sunsets of this planet. But I know better. I was watching. "Thanks, Mrs. Tran," I tell her.

"You're welcome. Good night, Justin. Say hello to your mom for me."

"I will." I hang up and fall back asleep and dream of the Christmas Murphy and I got a whole set of Star Wars guys and played with them all morning. Star Wars battles were the only ones me and Murphy were allowed to have. We never had toy guns or tanks or anything. You know those plastic army guys every kid in America plays with? Once, someone gave me a tube of them for my birthday and Dad threw them right in the garbage. Not the kitchen garbage either. He walked them all the way outside to the can in the alley, like he couldn't even stand to have them in the house.

In the dream, Dad's in his recliner, the color of the red-orange moon, reading a newspaper front to back. When he finishes, he starts another one. He pours another cup of coffee. Then a huge finger reaches down from a white flower moon and pushes the rewind button and holds it, so it will stop at the start of the scene and play it again. And again. And again.

■ ■ ■

Rodney didn't want to without a parent note, but he lets me off four stops early at Mom's work. I buy a bag of peanut M&M's (Mom's favorite) from a new guy working the register, and I'm thankful it's not Kathy, who always: (1) looks at me with panicked eyes, (2) reminds me she's known me since I was *this big,* (3) asks in a whisper how I'm doing but doesn't wait for the answer, (4) tells me how sick they all are over my dad, and (5) says how amazing Mom is for holding everything together. "A rock," she calls Mom. Or "a saint." Which is weird because Mom didn't choose this, and I always thought saints looked for trouble so they could prove themselves.

"Justin!" Mom says when I get to the pharmacy at

the back. Then her face goes pale and her hands stop in the middle of whatever she was doing. "Are you okay?"

I hold up the M&M's. "I got these. I thought if you have a break soon, you could watch me eat them. I mean, I could share them with you."

"That's so sweet. Thank you!" She hugs me across the counter. "But we're shorthanded and we're so far behind. Save me a few, okay?"

"Okay." I smile. "See you at home." I walk outside and sit on the curb and rip open the bag. I watch the parking lot, cars in and out. People hurrying or not. I eat five M&M's at one time.

"Hey." Mom sits down next to me.

"Hey! I thought you were busy."

"Yeah, well. Screw it. If I don't have five minutes to eat candy with my son, what kind of person am I?"

I smile and shake a few into her open hand, and we sit for a minute, crunching them. "These are so good," Mom says.

"I know. Why are you so far behind?"

"Because Tom, who thinks he knows everything, is a terrible manager."

I toss an M&M up and catch it in my mouth, like

Phuc and his oyster crackers. "So why don't you be the manager?"

Mom holds her hand out, and I shake out more M&M's into it. "I could seriously whip that place into shape. Like a navy ship, Justin. I'm telling you."

I laugh. "So why don't you?"

She smiles. "I'm just a tech. I'd have to go back to school for that."

"So why don't you?"

She looks at me like I make no sense, the same way I look at Mr. Lindberg in math every day. "Go back to school?" she asks.

"Yeah."

She goes blank, like her brain is making a billion calculations and her face is waiting for the result. Which is—the same smile she gives me when my church pants are suddenly too short and she realizes how fast I'm growing up.

"I appreciate your confidence," she says, "but I gotta send you and Murphy to school first."

I look down at the pavement and move the slush around with the toe of one shoe. "After that?" I ask.

"Maybe," Mom says, even though we both know the real answer.

. . .

Murphy is back on the couch after another shift, smelling like grease and watching the game. I sit down. The horn blows, and the players circle the ice and hop off.

"Did we win?" I ask.

"Nope, but we didn't lose. Yet. Tied going into overtime. The new guy at work threw away all the chicken, but I brought you some biscuits."

"Thanks." I eat a biscuit and watch the screen to figure out who we're playing. The Edmonton Oilers. "What's an Oiler?"

"Don't know. This is the third game in a row we've gone into overtime."

"Does that mean we're getting better?"

Murphy runs a hand through his sweaty hair. "Maybe. We can't get much worse. God, I stink."

The players skate back onto the ice. Five minutes lights up the clock. "What happens now?"

"Sudden death. First one to score wins."

"What if no one scores? Double overtime?" I think this is a thing, but I'm not sure and I wait for Murphy to laugh at me, but he doesn't.

"Nope. Just a tie. Why all the interest in hockey? You going out for the team next year?"

"Yeah, right. I can barely skate." The puck drops, and the players scramble and shove each other. "Just trying not to be useless at sports."

Murphy turns away from the TV and looks straight at me. He's got dark circles under his eyes that didn't used to be there. "You're not useless."

I shrug. Minnesota shoots and misses. "How old do you have to be to work at KFC?" I ask.

"Older than you. Don't even think about it. You're smart. You'll be riding in rockets one day. Or designing them. Or finding a cure for cancer."

"Not me. I couldn't dissect a sheep eye."

Murphy laughs. "Okay. The rocket thing, then."

We watch the game for a few minutes. A grass-green blur on the screen. I try to keep track of the puck. It's strange we can hear the sound of the skates scraping the ice, on our tiny TV. "I need to earn some money," I tell Murphy.

"For what?"

"I accidently asked a girl to get pizza with me."

The horn blows, and Murphy sighs. "Tied," he says. "Again."

"Better than losing, though, right?" I ask.

"Yeah, I guess. But sometimes it'd be nice to just get out there and crush it, you know? Like, go five–nothing. Instead of just barely making it. Every. Single. Time." I nod. Minnetonka High School just ended the worst hockey season anyone can remember. They were dead last in the conference, so they didn't even go to State. Everyone said how great Murphy did, pulling himself together so fast after Dad died. He only missed one game. His coach called him "indomitable," but Murphy didn't agree. He won't even talk about it. He pulls out his wallet and hands me a twenty. "Knock yourself out. Is she cute?"

The twenty feels thick between my fingers. "She's beautiful. And smart. And funny."

Murphy smiles. "Triple threat."

I hand the twenty back. "I don't want your money. I'll find some driveways to shovel. I was just asking."

But he won't take it back. "Little Monk, that's the best twenty bucks I've spent in a long time." He goes to take a shower, and I can hear him singing/yelling under the water. I stare at the twenty. I am very tired of being so helpless.

. . .

Mr. Sorenson says the worst thing teachers ever say, which is "Everyone, partner up." But actually I'm wrong. Because then he says, "We're doing an in-class assignment on Vietnam."

The word is a blade. It hits me and hacks up my insides. All the hair on my arms stands up and my whole body starts to sweat. Even my eyebrows. I'm pretty sure the whole class is looking at me, but I stare straight ahead so I won't have to know for sure.

Then something very weird happens. Brandon reaches across the aisle and grabs my shoulder. "I get Cease-Fire!" he yells.

"Dude!" Josh says from behind us. "What the heck?" But Brandon's nodding and smiling at me, so I just . . . smile back.

He scoots his desk over. "You're my ace in the hole, Cease-Fire."

"What?"

"You're smart. That's why we're partners."

Mr. Sorenson starts giving out the assignments, and my stomach turns into a pretzel and knots up tighter with each one. French occupation. The war's origin. The Vietcong.

"Ha! Bad luck for you," Brandon tells the pair next to us. "You got Charlie."

Mr. Sorenson clears his throat, which he does a lot when dealing with Brandon. "Mr. Engstrom and Mr. Olson. Tet Offensive."

"Tet a what?" Brandon asks, but Mr. Sorenson moves on. Gulf of Tonkin. My Lai Massacre. Lyndon B. Johnson.

I open my book, so Brandon does too. I turn the pages and stop on 72, so Brandon does too. "So let's just read the section," I say.

"Good idea."

I read, "The Tet Offensive was a series of surprise attacks by the Vietcong and North Vietnamese forces on cities and towns in South Vietnam." I'm shivering now, from all the sweat, but there's something else too. Something like wanting to beat this. To win. The way Murphy said it. I keep going. "'Tet' refers to the Vietnamese New Year, when traditionally a truce was observed."

"Hold on," Brandon says. "They attacked on a holiday? When they were supposed to have a truce?"

"Yeah, I guess."

"That's cold. Okay, my turn. 'It was considered to be a turning point in the Vietnam War.'" Brandon raises his eyebrows at me, like this is a fascinating development, and I laugh. "In-depth reporting on the Tet Offensive by the US media made clear to the American public that victory in Vietnam was not imminent. What's 'imminent'?"

"Soon."

"Well, that blows," Brandon says. "Your turn."

"Though US forces were quick to respond and regained much of the lost territory, the American public viewed the Tet Offensive as a sign of the undying North Vietnamese aggression and will," I say.

"They were tough," Brandon says, nodding like an old man remembering. "You gotta give 'em that."

I read, "At the end of the Tet Offensive, both sides had endured losses, and both sides claimed victory."

"Wait. What?" Brandon says.

I read it again. We stare at each other. "How does that work?" Brandon asks.

"I don't know."

Brandon shakes his head sadly, an old man again. "Cease-Fire," he says, "war is so messed up."

. . .

I've been on the bench for twenty minutes and I can't feel my toes. Part of me wants to go home, but more of me wants to stay in case Benny H. comes. I want to know more about the Indians and the lake and the burial mounds. For example, Were the bodies all buried together? Was everybody buried there, or just important people, like the chiefs? And is the town of Mound across the lake *that* kind of mound?

We didn't even finish burying Dad. We left his coffin at the bottom of a hole with a mound of black dirt beside it. Next to some fake flowers on a tripod. After Pastor Steve gave a speech about him, when they'd only met one time. Or maybe twice. Is that how we felt about Dad? Is that the best we could do? Toss down a few dinky handfuls of dirt and walk away? And why did we do that anyway? Mrs. Peterson is always talking about *symbolism* in English, and it seems like throwing dirt onto someone's coffin should *symbolize* something. But what? I looked over my shoulder the whole way to the car, tripping over gravestones, because it was so weird to just leave Dad like that.

Who would shovel the dirt over him? Would it be that night? The next day? The next week?

And here's something even weirder: we haven't been back since. Mom says it's too cold, and plus the stone hasn't come in yet. She says we'll go in the spring. Maybe she's afraid to see him like that. Covered with dirt (I hope), then snow, and surrounded by bare branches and ribbons ripped up by the wind. Maybe it would be too much for her. In the spring, there'll be daffodils and budding trees and robins hopping around in the grass. But Dad will still be dead. No matter how much the birds chirp and build their nests and look ahead.

■ ■ ■

The waitress already brought me another Sprite and I'm too embarrassed to ask if there's free refills, so I'm trying to drink as slow as possible, but it's almost to the bottom because there's nothing else to do. I can't look around at the other people because it's too embarrassing, and staring into space makes me seem like a freak. I'm also trying not to check my watch too much, but I check it again. Jenni's seven minutes late. I can't picture waiting much longer, but I also can't picture paying for my Sprite (or Sprites) and walking across the whole Pizza Hut with everyone watching me.

"Hey. I'm *so* sorry." Jenni slides onto the bench across from me and fills up everything, my whole vision, like a human snowflake blooming from nothing. Her blond hair peeks out from a white fluffy hat, and her coat is light blue with white fur. Her cheeks are pink and her eyes are bright. It's like she injected the air with extra oxygen. I can breathe again. I picture all the molecules, floating around on their backs, fat and happy. She smiles, and I realize she's actually smiling back at me because I'm grinning at her like a nut job. "My brother's afraid of his boots," she says.

"What?"

"That's why we're late! My mom told my brother to get his boots on, and he threw a hissy fit because he said they try to eat his feet."

I laugh. I can't believe she's here, across from me. I can't believe this second is so opposite from the last one. From the last billion. I want to touch her sleeve, just to make sure I'm seeing it right, but I'm also trying very, very hard to be cool. "How old is he?"

"Two. Do you have a little brother? Or sister?"

"Nope. Just an older brother."

"Lucky. I'm starving. Did you order?" I shake my head. "Do you like pepperoni?" I nod. The waitress comes, and Jenni orders a pepperoni pizza and a Mountain Dew, which she sucks through the straw for as long as she can. Then she sits back and catches her breath. "My mom hates this stuff!" she says.

"Yeah?"

She nods. "But I love it. It's like you can feel it going right into your bloodstream."

"Yeah." *Say something besides "yeah."* "Hey, I'm sorry I didn't take you to the dance."

Jenni shrugs. "It was kind of lame. And it was *so loud* that I still had this, like, buzzing in my head when I fell asleep. I literally dreamed I was a bee in a hive all night. And I wasn't even the queen, so that sucked." I laugh. "So this is way better," Jenni says, sucking up more Mountain Dew. "'Cause we can talk."

And she does. And her voice turns the color up

around us, like adjusting that button on the TV to fix green faces and pale streets. The bench is crimson now. The lights are gold. The snow glitters outside. Jenni's hands dance with her stories, and she makes a million faces, and once I laugh so hard Sprite comes out my nose.

"Hey," I interrupt her, before I chicken out. "You're really cool."

She tucks her hair behind her ears. "Thanks. You're really cool too."

"But I don't mean, like, you're just cool. You're like . . . Being with you is like . . . Being with you is like being inside of sunlight. Like the sparkliest kind of sunlight."

Jenni blushes, and I do too. Then she says, "Oh! I almost forgot. I brought you something." She digs in her bag and hands me a book called *Animal Farm*. "It's our last book club book for the year. Discussion starts April first. I got you a copy. Just in case."

"Seriously?"

"Yeah. I mean, you know, my mom did."

"I can pay her for it."

Jenni rolls her eyes. "Earth to Justin. Hello? It's a gift? I haven't started it yet, but it looks pretty weird."

"Perfect."

Jenni laughs. "Yeah. Exactly."

. . .

The one good thing about math is unassigned seats, so I can sit next to Phuc, who explains everything in a language I understand. Unlike Mr. Lindberg, who speaks in a foreign language that only Phuc understands. Phuc is my translator.

"Here's what I want to know," I say to Phuc.

He raises his eyebrows.

"Say there are different versions of us in the different dimensions."

"What about the function of x?"

"Screw the function of x. As far as I can tell, x has no function."

"Justin," Mr. Lindberg says. "Language." That man has radar for "language."

"Sorry," I tell him, then turn back to Phuc. "So different versions of us in ten dimensions. Can they communicate with each other?"

"I doubt it."

"But it's possible."

Phuc smiles at me. "That's what's so freaking amazing about physics, Justin. We don't even know what's possible!"

"Yeah, yeah, okay. So obviously, we don't know how to communicate with the other dimensions. You and me, I mean. But what if ourselves, or other people, in the other dimensions are communicating with us?"

Phuc nods. "Like I said, anything's possible. You know what my mom says?"

"What?"

"Venture all. See what fate brings. She says it's a Vietnamese proverb, but I think she got it off a Hallmark card." Phuc tips his head to the right. "But you know what? Maybe it doesn't matter."

■ ■ ■

I'm sitting on the couch after school but the TV's off, so I just see my own reflection blurred on the screen, which freaks me out (it doesn't take much), so I move down a cushion to Murphy's spot. But I can still see myself, so I close my eyes and focus on what I'm doing. Which I will never tell anyone about as long as I live. Which is listening. For Dad. In some other dimension. I don't know what I think I'll hear. A message? A pulse in the atmosphere? Dad's ghost, the old-fashioned way, rattling some chains around?

It doesn't last long because I start to fall asleep. I feel the drift, like rocking on a small boat under sun lowering down, waiting on the crappies to bite. Then it's more like a pull, and I'm underwater. But it's not sleep, it's memory. I look up and see the sun, greenish through the lake. Then a black shadow. I'm sinking but I can't yell. The water throbs, once. I'm still going down. My arms fight but they're heavy. Then everything turns white. I'm lying in the bottom of the boat and I spread my fingers out like a frog. Sound comes back but I didn't know it was missing. I can hear the water lap against the boat and a man choking. Or crying? Dad picks me up. We are both shivering and dripping. Only us. It's only us in the boat. Dad sets me on his lap facing his chest, the way you do spider on the swing, the way you hold a baby. *But I'm not a baby,* I think, and start to cry because I remember now, leaning too far. *Maybe I am a baby.* Dad wraps his arms around me and puts his forehead right on mine, and we stay like that for a very long time. Then

Dad starts the motor. The sun is touching the tree-tops, and the water looks magical under the orange light. Dad holds me with one arm and drives with the other, all the way back to the dock.

Real sleep is pulling me now. I've never seen that memory before. I must have been terrified in the water, but the feel of it—what's the word? Tenor. The tenor of the memory is love. The world darkens to charcoal, and right before I go under, I think, *So that's something.*

CHAPTER FIVE

I can see Benny H.'s top hat from two blocks away, and I start running, like when I saw Jenni alone in the hall. It's a bad idea, since I'm still trying to be invisible in Wicapi, but some people are just worth running for. He startles when I catch up to him, then takes his pipe out of his mouth and says, "Oh. Hello. I thought I might see you today. I had a hunch. And I always believe my hunches."

"Me too," I say. But I don't tell him about the hunch I had the night Dad died. We didn't play Scrabble because I was studying for a math final. It was three days until Christmas break. Mom called to tell Dad to defrost the chicken. So he did. And I looked up at him, at his back, as he watched the raw chicken turn under the yellow light, and the microwave counting down. Four, three, two, one. It beeped and he took the plate out and set it on the counter. Then he tipped his head toward the door and lifted two fingers to his mouth to tell me he was going out for smokes, and went to get his coat. When he opened the door to leave, I looked up, even though I was in the middle of multiplying a fraction and would lose my place and have to start over. And I knew it was the last time I'd see him alive.

Mom came home and started cooking the chicken. She wasn't worried. Sometimes Dad got his smokes and walked around the lake. Mom asked me, "Broccoli or squash?" and I said "Neither," and she stuck her tongue out at me. Then the phone rang. And I knew. It could've been anyone calling about anything, but I knew. Mom picked up the phone and tucked it against her shoulder since her hands were wet. Then she gasped and the phone slid out. It swung down on its curly cord and smashed against the kitchen floor, and that's the last thing I remember until the hospital. That plastic smash. Like I said, that night goes in and out.

Benny H. is watching me through the smoke between us. And I realize for the first time that he might know who I am. That I'm *that kid.* "Want to sit on the bench?" I ask.

"I'd like nothing more," he says, and we walk toward it together. He puffs on his pipe, and I suck the smoke into my lungs. It's a comfortable smell. Like butter in a frying pan or a Pop-Tart in the toaster. We get to the bench and sit. The houses are off the lake because the ice is getting thinner, and the surface is an empty white sheet, pulled tight.

"Tell me more about the lake," I say. "And the Indians."

"Well, the lake was full of fish, of course. You got your pike, paddlefish, sturgeon, bass, sunnies of course, bullheads. But also wild rice, which was a staple of the Indian diet." He turns and looks at me. "You know, it's better to use their real name. Let's say 'Dakota.' Okay with you?" I nod. "So at the end of the summer, early September, let's say, the Dakota would take their canoes into the shallows of the lake in the very early morning and harvest the rice."

"Wait. How do you know all this?"

"What do you mean, how do I know it? I read books. Don't you?"

"Yeah, I do. I'm in book club at school. Or, I was."

Benny H. nods. "Good. I spend most of my time at the library."

I almost say, *I know that about you,* but I don't want him to say what he knows about me. "Is there any left?" I ask.

"Dakota? Or wild rice?"

"Either."

Benny H. puffs on his pipe. "Not on this lake."

I look out at the blank lake and think of riding Murphy's friend's snowmobile, smelling diesel and cutting fresh tracks in the snow and feeling the moonlight on my shoulders. I shiver for no reason, which Grandma always said means someone just walked across your grave, but I think it's the opposite. I think I just walked across the Dakota's graves. I think we're all walking across the Dakota's graves all the time and don't even realize it. I squint at the lake but it stays silent, like it knows too but won't say anything. Benny H.'s smoke keeps blowing toward it, sometimes in clouds and sometimes rings, disappearing before it gets there.

. . .

I'm trying to get to the library before first period so I'm walking fast but I'm also trying not to draw attention to myself, which is extremely hard to do. I pass the special ed class where Brandon's dropping his sister off. I knew he had a sister in that class, but I never really thought about them together. They don't seem like they're part of the same universe.

"You don't have to walk me every day. I can do it myself," she tells him. She's only a year younger, but she's small and he's huge, so when she talks to him, she has to look up.

"I know you can," Brandon says. "I'm just making sure you don't skip school and spend the whole day at Dairy Queen."

She laughs in a loud burst, like confetti. "I wouldn't do that!" she says.

Brandon shakes his head like he's not sure. "I don't know . . ."

"I like the Oreo Blizzards," she says.

"I know you do."

"I love you, big bro!" his sister says, and throws her arms around his waist.

"Jeez, you're strong. You been lifting weights?"

She confetti-laughs again and lets go. "Study hard!" she tells him.

Brandon turns to go. "I always do," he says.

"Yeah, right!" she yells at his back, giggling.

Brandon shakes his head. "See what I go through?" he asks the special ed teacher, and she grins at him.

Mr. Sorenson says history is like a prism, because you see different things depending on which side you look through. The trick, he told us, is to look through as many sides as you can. Watching Brandon, I think people must be like that too.

"Hey, Cease-Fire."

I'm standing in the middle of the hall with kids moving around me, like a rock in a river, and also my mouth is open like a frog. I close it. Then I open it again and say, "Hey."

"You going my way?" Brandon asks.

"Huh?"

He points up the hallway. "Are you going this way?"

"Oh. Yeah."

So we walk together, and I picture everyone as prisms, bouncing their rainbow lights all over the hall. It's the opposite of using faraway points, and for the first time since Dad died, I can see everything I've been missing. Plus, almost everyone says hey to Brandon or yells some nickname at him or at least nods. It's like I slipped into some other dimension of junior high. Like I'm seeing one of the little dimensions Phuc says are tucked into the big one.

"Where you headed?" Brandon asks.

"The library."

"Figures." He knocks his shoulder into me and I almost fall, but the wall catches me. "You know what books I like?" he asks. I shake my head. "Those ones by that guy with all the crazy made-up words and the drawings. You know? He wrote *The Twits.* That's my favorite."

"Roald Dahl?"

"Yeah, that's him! I guess that's kids' stuff to you."

"No. I like those books too."

Brandon smiles at me, then turns in to his English class. "See ya, Cease-Fire."

"See ya."

. . .

Murphy's got a migraine, which sucks, but it means he's in bed at the same time as me, which never, ever happens. He's lying on his back in the gray shadows, with a towel over his eyes. "You need some medicine?" I ask.

"I took some."

"Water?"

"Nope."

"Okay." We lie there, quiet. "We're learning about Vietnam in history," I say for no reason.

"Oh yeah?"

"Yeah." I can't think of anything else to say. I try to figure out if the dark feels cozy or prickly, but it's hard to tell.

"Mom told me once that no one really welcomed the soldiers home from Vietnam," Murphy says. I turn my head to face him, even though I can only see his outline. "People were so against the war they didn't say thank you or even ask what it was like over there. So the soldiers had to just, like, try to walk back into normal life again, you know? After all they'd been through. With no one wanting to talk about it, Mom said."

He takes the towel off and stares straight up, at the ceiling.

"I told Dad once, I said, 'Dad, I'm sorry nobody gave you the respect you deserved when you came home from Vietnam. I'm sorry you didn't get a parade.'" My eyes go wide in the dark, like an alley cat. I can't imagine ever saying those words to Dad. Bringing the war up on purpose. To his face. But Murphy was always braver than me.

"You know what he said?" Murphy asks. "'Nothing I did deserved a parade.'"

∎ ∎ ∎

Mr. Sorenson is calling us to his desk one by one, in alphabetical order, and I'm watching the black hand of the clock tick closer to the two. He's on "Nelson" and there's still "Norberg" before me, so I might get out of here before I have to tell him I don't have a *formulated idea* for my National History Project. Or an idea at all. He calls Norberg. Two more minutes. No way he'll get to— "Mr. Olson," he says.

I sit on the folding chair next to his desk and tuck

my feet under it. "So," he says. "Tell me about your idea."

"Um, well. I don't really . . . I'm not totally sure. Yet."

Mr. Sorenson taps his pen on his open notebook. I can see the list of ideas next to all the names up to mine. Israel-Palestine. The Berlin Wall. Apartheid. "Well, tell me some of the contenders."

"I was thinking about doing something on the war."

"Which war?"

"Desert Storm."

Mr. Sorenson tips his head from side to side, thinking about it. "What about doing a previous war? You'd find more material. You could do the cold war, or just the Cuban Missile Crisis. That was a turning point. Or Vietnam."

The word lights up like a flare between us and hangs there, waiting for me to do something. Mr. Sorenson's face is blank. He hasn't heard the whispers in the hall? Is that possible?

"I don't think so," I tell him. "I actually . . . I changed my mind. I want to do . . ." I look at the clock. One minute left. "Wicapi."

"Wicapi? The town?"

"Yeah. It's my hometown, so . . ."

Mr. Sorenson tips his head to one side again, but doesn't tip it back this time. So I guess he's not considering this one. "Right, but the assignment is about conflict. I just don't know how you would do that."

I smile. "I do."

. . .

Every time I try to wave to Murphy, Mom bats my hand down, like she does to Axl Rose when she tries to knock ornaments off the Christmas tree.

"Mom! Seriously! Why do you think I've been begging you to bring me to KFC?"

She eats a bite of coleslaw. I have no idea why. I didn't think anyone ate the coleslaw. "I thought you liked the food," she says.

"Please. I eat this chicken practically every night. The whole point is to embarrass Murphy."

"Yeah, well. Not happening."

I sigh and stir my mashed potatoes around, trying to drown them in the gravy puddle. I flick my hand up like I'm going to wave and Mom flinches, and I laugh. She smacks my hand, but she's laughing too, which is good to hear.

"Did you know that in France 'KFC' is 'PFK' for 'Poulet Frit Kentucky'? That's the only good thing I've learned in French all year," I tell her. *"C'est vrai."*

Mom shakes her head. "Justin. You are one interesting bird."

"Mom, please." I cover my drumstick with one hand and whisper, "No bird jokes in front of the chicken."

She smiles, but her face looks tired from trying so hard. I eat my biscuit and watch Murphy at the register (without waving). He still has a little of his sunbeam smile, and he flashes what's left of it at the customers. He chats with them and high-fives some and gives the little kids the thumbs-up.

"Murphy's good at this job," I tell Mom.

"Murphy is a junior in high school," Mom says. "He should be at baseball practice. Like a regular kid."

I open my mouth to ask how she can actually expect him to be a regular kid after everything, but Murphy slides in next to me in the red plastic booth and knocks me over. "Enjoying your KFC experience?" he asks.

Mom grins at him, like it was a serious question. "Couldn't be better!" she says.

"Awesome," Murphy says.

I roll my eyes at both of them. "Murph. You should be mayor of Wicapi when you grow up," I tell him. "You know everyone in this place."

He smiles. "Nah, not me."

"Okay, fine, pro hockey star."

But he shakes his head. "No, I'll do something easy. Construction, prob'ly."

"That doesn't sound easy," I say, but Murphy doesn't hear me. He's looking out the window like he can see his future hanging around in the parking lot. He's not frowning, exactly, but it's close.

■ ■ ■

"What's your problem, Olson?" Mitchell shoves me against the wall. So today's the day.

"I—"

"I'm so sick of you walking around like you're

better than everyone." He moves his tongue around in his mouth like he might spit on me. Kids start to crowd in, and I can see Phuc at the edge. His face is blotchy with fear, and he opens his mouth, but I shake my head at him, just a tiny shake. But Mitchell sees it, like a piranha detecting a single drop of blood in the water. "What?" he snarls. "You got something to say?" He's got me by the arms, and he slams me again.

The thud of my head against the wall reminds me of when Mom backed into a telephone pole in the grocery store parking lot a few weeks after Dad died. It was dusk, and shadowy and slippery, and we heard that sick bump. "Crap!" she whispered. "Crap, crap, crap." We got out and looked at the busted taillight and the dent. It was snowing huge pretty flakes, and the air was warm like it is sometimes when it snows. Did you know that in Minnesota, it can get too cold to snow? Truth. And the word that came into my head was "mercy."

There was something about how soft the snow was, and the air like velvet, and that it was just a taillight (not a person) and the car wasn't wrecked. I was okay. Mom was okay. Just the mercy that we were both still alive, still here.

We got back in the car, but Mom didn't drive it. We just sat, watching the snow fall. I tried to see the design of each flake before it melted on the windshield. Mom said, "If Dad were here, he would fix that light." Her voice had tears in it. "He would say 'Easy fix' and go to the shop and get the part. Or if the toilet broke, he'd just go to the hardware store and get the . . . What's the word I'm looking for?" She looked at me, and there were so many tears in the bottoms of her eyes that one blink made them spill over. I shrugged, helpless. I don't know anything about toilets. "The flange," Mom whispered, looking back out the windshield. "He could fix anything," she said to the falling snow. "I should have told him that. I should have told him how good he was. How much money it saved us. How much I appreciated it."

"You did," I said, and she turned to me.

"Did what?"

"You did tell him he was good at fixing stuff. You told him all those things you just said. You did tell him."

She blinked again. More tears fell. "Did I?" I nodded, and she smiled. She reached over and squeezed my hand, and I let her. I could still feel the word floating around the car. Mercy.

"Look at me when I'm talking to you, Olson!"

I blink, like Mom did, but lucky for me, I'm not crying. Yet. I'm still pinned to the wall. My feet are dangling, and please, God, don't let me pee my pants.

"That's your problem. You think you're too good for all of us. Even though your dad . . ."

My head's tilted, so I see Brandon coming before Mitchell does and before I can decide what that means, Brandon grabs Mitchell and yanks him back. I fall down from the wall and land in a crouch but stay on my feet even though every muscle is jelly. Small victories. "What's wrong with you, Jergen?" Brandon asks. He's got Mitchell by the shirt and a hockey player on each side. Mitchell is silent. He looks away. "I'm gonna let you go," Brandon says, "but if I ever see you picking on Olson again, you're done. Got it?" He lets go, and Mitchell walks off like he doesn't care, like Axl Rose after Mom chases her off the counter.

"You okay, Cease-Fire?" Brandon reaches his hand down and I take it. I'm still crouching, which is super embarrassing. He pulls me up and fixes my shirt on my shoulders like Mom does before church. "I hate bullies," he says, and the two hockey players nod. One says, "That dude's such a poser." Then some teachers are coming and everyone takes off before they start handing out pink slips. I watch Brandon and his buddies walk away, and the word hangs on. Mercy.

■ ■ ■

Benny H. is down the block when I get off the bus and I start to walk toward him but slow down when I get closer. He's walking in a tiny circle, like looking for something. His huge black coat makes him look like a black crow in a gray world. Gray sky, gray wind, gray smoke from his pipe, and he's muttering at the gray sidewalk. I start to turn around, but then I think of how fast Brandon came toward me. How he didn't hesitate. And I keep walking toward Benny H.

"Hey," I say when I get to him, and he glances up like I'm a stranger passing by. "It's really cold," I say. "You want to get a cup of coffee?" I have no idea how I'll make this happen because I have no money. But Benny H. keeps walking in his circle. "Did you lose something?" I ask, even though there's only ice and salt on the ground, between Benny H.'s black boots and my beat-up sneakers. He's still muttering, and it sounds like the same word repeated but I can't tell what word. "Can I walk you to the library?" I ask.

He finally stops and looks at me. There are tears in his eyes that might be from the cold but might not be. "Time to go," he tells me.

"Go where?"

"Home."

"Okay. Can I walk you?"

He shakes his head. "No, no. I'll walk you."

So we walk to my apartment building, and he waves his arm up and down like he can wave me up to the second floor. "Are you sure?" I ask. "Will you be okay out here?" He laughs his Jolly Green Giant laugh and waves me up again. I take the steps two at a time and unlock the apartment door and run to the living room window to look out. Benny H. is walking back up the sidewalk. He passes the spot where he got stuck in the circle and takes a left at the comic shop corner and disappears into the gray air.

. . .

The librarian keeps adding books to the stacks on my table and saying stuff like, "I thought about looking under 'American Indian'" and "This one's on Great Lakes history, but you can look in the index" and "I just remembered this one on early Minnesota towns." Each time she's more excited, and I can't figure it out because she was always the crabbiest one when they'd march us all downtown in elementary school to get our library cards. Maybe it was just too many kids at once. Dad was like that. He'd hide in the bedroom when the Iowa cousins came for Christmas Eve or it was Mom's turn to host Bunco.

I start flipping through the books and taking notes and marking the ones with good pictures with little scraps of paper like battle flags. And pretty soon I get why she's so excited. Because this is so different from studying other history. Different from Plymouth Rock and the colonies and throwing tea into the harbor. Because this is our place. All the things we forgot about. All the things we used to know. Right in front of us if we bother to look.

"Hi," Mom says. She sits down across from me, and I stare at her until I remember I wrote *at the library* on a sticky note and left it on the kitchen table.

Last month I went to Phuc's after school (like I did a million times before Dad died), and she freaked out when she got home and I wasn't there and no one answered at Phuc's (probably his sisters were louder than the phone ringing). I walked in the door literally the second before she started calling every kid in seventh grade looking for me. She had the student directory in her hand! Death does weird things to the living.

"Hi, Mom. What are you doing here?"

"I saw your note. Thank you for leaving it, by the way."

"You're welcome by the way."

"And I thought I'd come and see if you needed help."

"Oh. Thanks. I don't really."

"Can I help anyway?"

I smile. "Sure."

"Great!" She actually pushes up her sleeves. I shake my head. "What?"

"Nothing."

"What can I do?"

"Um, I'm looking for anything on the Dakota on Lake Minnetonka or in Wicapi or anywhere around here. And on their life in Minnesota. And on the founding of Wicapi."

Mom raises her eyebrows. "Wow."

"Yeah. It's for our National History Project on conflict. Mr. Sorenson hates my idea. He thinks I should do an actual war."

Mom picks up a book and flips to the index. "Yeah, well. I'm sure to the Dakota it was an actual war."

Then I just reach across the table and hug her. In the middle of the library. Because she's so good at saying the perfect thing and sometimes I forget I have her. Sometimes I go to junior high and Mitchell pins me to the wall, and Mom goes to work and church and counts pills and prays, and Murphy goes to high school and KFC, and we all just forget. And then a moment like this comes. And we sit in the middle of our own history. And we remember.

CHAPTER SIX

"You got homework?" Murphy asks. My mouth is full of taco, so I shake my head. Mom had to work late, so Murphy took me to Kmart for new gym shoes, then drove through Taco Bell. "You wanna go home?" he asks.

"No way," I say through my taco.

"You want to just drive around?"

"Yeah."

So we drive. Murphy's heater only goes on high, so he blasts it and cracks the windows and the car is hot and cold and smells like meat and peaches from Murphy's air freshener that's shaped like a tree and makes me wonder about people who live where peach trees grow. Do they have pine-smelling trees in their cars and wonder about us?

There's tons of traffic and nothing good on the radio, but there's nowhere I'd rather be, including Florida (orange trees), which is where I almost always want to be. Mom took us down there once to visit her mom, and she spent the whole trip home saying how she'd never go back to Florida. I was super bummed but didn't say so because Mom was even more bummed about how *some things never change.* I was only five, but I remember sitting on the white sand and staring at the turquoise water and not understanding why everyone didn't live in Florida. I still don't really.

"Let's go around the lake," Murphy says. So we wind around and I eat another taco and watch the moonlight flicker on the cold, dark ice.

"You ever want to live anywhere else?" I ask Murphy.

"No. Why?"

"I don't know. I was just thinking about Florida."

Murphy smiles. "Be good to visit, I guess. But there's no hockey."

"Oh. Right. Did you know that in the Dakota

language they have, like, sixteen different verbs for 'home'? Like, 'coming home,' 'returning home,' 'bringing something home'?"

"Makes sense to me," Murphy says.

"How come?"

"I mean, I don't know, home is pretty important. What would we be without home?" Murphy slows down at a yellow light. We stop. We wait. We start to move again. "It must have been so sad for them," Murphy says.

"What?"

"To love home so much, and then lose it."

"Yeah." Sometimes Murphy surprises me. "Murph?"

"What?"

"Can you do me a favor?"

"Anything, Monk."

I take a deep breath. "Can you find out what happened when Dad died?"

Murphy swallows. I can tell because he has a lump in his throat that moves up and down like Dad's. When did that happen? "What do you mean?" he asks.

"I mean, like, what happened? Did he walk out on the tracks? Did he fall? I just want to know."

Murphy stares straight ahead. "Okay," he says slowly. "And how would I find that out?"

"I don't know. Ask around? You know everyone."

"*Ask around?* What, I'm like, 'Hi, would you like to try the new spicy hot wings? And by the way, you know Larry Olson? The guy who got killed on the train tracks? Do you happen to know anything about that? I'm his son. This isn't weird or anything. I just want to know.'"

I sigh, and look back out at the lake. "Yeah, I guess." Murphy curves the car along the shoreline. The lights are bright on the other side. Big houses. Rich families. Alive dads. "So, what? We just never know?" I ask.

"What difference does it make?"

"Are you kidding? It makes all the difference!"

"Monk. He's dead either way."

"Yeah. I know."

. . .

The snow didn't gear up this time. Usually it falls slow at first so you can get home, stop at the grocery store, whatever. Not today. It's like it all collected in the clouds and then God (or Jesus or whoever is in charge up there—probably no one, the way things are looking down here) just pulled the lever and released it. Dumped it all, the way the M&M's pour out of that machine at the rich grocery store where we only go on Kentucky Derby day because they sell fresh mint that Mom needs to make those drinks she likes. Her dad was from Kentucky.

They let us out of school at noon, and I feel off-balance seeing Rodney this early in the day and he's off-balance too. The radio's off and he keeps looking in the rearview mirror like we might be endangering ourselves in some new way he hasn't thought of. He's got both hands on the wheel like an old lady and his wipers on so high they squeak. I punch his shoulder, but soft, before I get off.

"Last stop," I tell him. "You made it."

Rodney lets out all his breath, like the snow cloud and the M&M machine. "I hate driving in snow. My older brother. Got in a huge wreck on a day like this. He was never the same. My whole family was never the same." He shakes a cigarette out of a crushed white pack and lights it, and his hands are trembling.

"And here I am driving all these little lives around. Too precious. Too precious for me."

"I didn't know you smoked."

He blows the smoke sideways, out the cracked window into the falling snow. "Only on days like this."

"Well, you did good, Rodney."

He nods. "Thanks, little man. You're the coolest." He holds up his hand for a high five, and I smack it. He pulls the lever and the door swings open and I stomp down into the snow, which, despite freaking Rodney out, is totally amazing, how fast and heavy it's falling, like grieving. (I should tell that to the social worker. She'd probably appreciate it.)

I walk down the white sidewalk through the white world (you can't even see the lake, the snow is so thick) and up the steps to the apartment, and just as I unlock the door, there's a sizzle and pop and the power goes out. Inside, the rooms are filled with snow light, which is an impossible color to describe because in reality it's gray, but it's the most beautiful gray and it lights up from the inside and there's no word for that. I sit down on the couch and Axl Rose climbs into my lap. I close my eyes and listen for Dad, but all I hear is Axl Rose purring, which at this second is enough.

. . .

"Whoa," Phuc says when he walks in. I'm in the middle of my bed surrounded by stacks of library books. They take up every possible space. There's even one on my pillow. "That's a lot of books," Phuc says, and bounces onto Murphy's empty bed. He clicks on Murphy's lava lamp and watches the lava float and bounce in its purple sea. "Where'd your brother get this thing?"

"Some girl gave it to him for his birthday."

"His girlfriend?"

"Huh?" I look up.

"The girl who gave it to him. Is she his girlfriend?" Phuc asks.

"I don't know. I don't think so." I look back down.

"Are you failing history or something?"

"No. Why?"

Phuc pulls his backpack onto Murphy's bed and

unzips it. He pulls out his math book. "I've never seen you so . . . obsessed."

"Yeah. I know." But I don't know, really. I have no idea why I'm working this hard. I have triple the sources I need. I had to ask Mr. Sorenson for extra of those note-taking sheets. Plus I have an A-minus in history already and this is only 25 percent of our grade.

Axl Rose jumps into a centimeter of space on my bed and then sprawls out on the book I'm reading. I push her off, but Phuc calls her over. He loves cats, but one of his sisters is allergic. He scratches her head until she purrs; then he opens his book and starts his homework. For a while we work without talking. Axl Rose falls asleep on Murphy's pillow. Phuc stops every few minutes to watch the lava. "I wish some girl would give me one of these for my birthday," he says. He puts his math book away and pulls out geography.

I turn the page of a massive book that's so musty it made my whole backpack stink, and I see a black-and-white picture of Spirit Knob, when it existed. Some men are pulling a sailboat onto the shore, and one man's already standing on the sand, looking out at the camera instead of up at the most sacred place on the lake. But probably he doesn't know that. And something clicks, like when Dad used to fix the chain on my dirt bike. "This!" I say, too loud, and Phuc looks at me like I've finally lost it, and also like he expected it. Axl Rose lifts her head and puts it back down, uninterested.

I turn the book around and point to the highest tree on Spirit Knob. "This is the reason I'm obsessed."

"That tree?"

"Yeah. I mean, not just that, but all of it. Like, all this stuff happened on this lake, and we live here and we don't even know about it. This place isn't even here anymore. It's under some tennis courts." I turn the page and point to a picture taken from the top of Spirit Knob, looking down, like the view God has, or used to have. "There were six hundred burial mounds in Wicapi. And now there's zero. All these books"— I pick one up and toss it back down—"are full of the way things used to be. People who used to be. And no one remembers them."

Phuc blinks and leans forward a little, watching me basically the same way he watched the lava.

"And I just think it . . . matters." Dad slides into

my head. He's sitting at the kitchen table. Silent, with his glass of Jack Daniel's, one quarter full. War in his head. Death seeped into all the cracks of his brain, into all his memories, taking over. "We all go around like nothing bad ever happened," I tell Phuc. "Like there's not millions of bones under us and ghosts all around us. We just go out waterskiing!" Dad, dead on the tracks. I see it as a memory even though I wasn't there. And new soldiers on TV, young ones, and the president saying words like "liberation." "I just think someone should remember," I tell Phuc, and he smiles.

"Guess that's gonna be you."

∎ ∎ ∎

It's my third time in church in a week (Palm Sunday, Lenten Soup, Good Friday) but at least the end (Easter) is in sight, which I guess for Jesus was just the beginning. (If Mom had made me go on Maundy Thursday, this would've been my fourth time. But I said I'd only go if she could tell me what Maundy Thursday is. Which she couldn't.) I swear I'll never be happier to hear those trumpets blast my eardrums and sit squished in a pew full of perfume and drooly babies in white suits. Unless the church has some new thing planned for Pentecost. God, I hope not.

The lights are dim and the cross is draped in black, which makes the song "Back in Black" pop into my head. *I've been looking at the sky 'cause it's gettin' me high. Forget the hearse 'cause I never die.* I start to laugh, thinking about Jesus rocking an electric guitar at the front of the church, but I bite my lip in time. Even Pastor Steve looks appropriately sad tonight. Not as sad as he looked when Dad died, but I guess he's more used to Jesus dying, since he does it every year.

Mom's been dabbing her eyes with a tissue the whole service, which makes me want to scream because she's cried about Jesus more than she's cried about Dad, as far as I can tell, and what did Jesus ever do for her? I mean, at least Dad went to work and fixed stuff. Plus Jesus is going to rise in like two days, and Dad never will. Dad's at the bottom of a grave that (hopefully) someone filled with dirt after we left.

I stare at the dark stained-glass window over the piano, where Moses stands on a mountain holding the Ten Commandments and think of *Animal Farm*. I started reading it last night in case I decide to go back to book club on Monday (which I probably won't, because Mrs. Peterson will make me *raise a salient point,* and I don't have one). In the book there's a raven named Moses who tells all the animals that when they die, they'll go to Sugarcandy Mountain, up in the sky. Sugarcandy Mountain is full of clover and sugar and every day is Sunday (barf). So the animals keep killing themselves with work so they can get there when they're dead. It sounds so totally and obviously bogus to me.

Finally church ends and I wait for Mom to do whatever she does afterwards, and when she comes back to the pew, all the sniffling people are gone and it's just me. She sits down. She seems thinner. Or her hair seems thinner. I don't know. "Ready?" she asks. "Or do you need a minute?"

"Mom. Would you be mad if I didn't believe in heaven?" I ask.

Her eyes get big, but Mom has a killer poker face, and she puts it on quick. "Of course not. Dad and I always said, you and Murphy are free to believe whatever you want to believe."

"I just think heaven . . . I just think it sounds like

something that's supposed to make us feel better. About dying. So we picture angels and clouds and harps instead of worms eating our flesh until we're bones and then the bones turning to dust." Mom clears her throat. "Sorry."

She shakes her head. "No, I get it. But you know, heaven is supposed to be for souls. Not bodies."

"Phuc says we exist at all times of our life in other dimensions."

Mom nods. "I like the sound of that."

"Yeah. Me too. I just don't know how to . . . picture him."

"Who? Jesus?"

"Mom! No!"

"Sorry! I just . . . You were looking at the cross, so . . ." She drops her voice a little. "How to picture Dad?"

"Yes."

We sit for a minute, still staring at the cross, which has nothing to do with anything, but it's just where we look. Then Mom says, "You know my favorite way to picture Dad?" I shake my head. "On the day you came home from the hospital, Dad fell asleep in his chair with you in one arm and Murphy in the other.

And he didn't call out or jerk awake or sweat or even move. After a while he just . . . opened his eyes. And smiled at me. And it was the most content I ever saw him. The most peaceful. That's what I like to picture. I hope if he's in another dimension, like Phuc says, he's living that moment a lot."

"Yeah." My voice comes out like a tired ghost. "Me too."

. . .

Murphy's tapping his fingers on the steering wheel and looking at the church door every seven seconds.

"Where *is* she?" he asks.

"In the church," I say.

"Duh."

"You *asked.* What's your problem anyway? You got somewhere to be? 'Cause, you know, it's like, Easter Sunday. Family. Baskets. Big fluffy bunny. Ring a bell?"

"Shut up, Justin. What's eating you?"

"*Me?* I'm minding my own business. You're the one acting like a junkie."

Murphy laughs. "You know all about that, right? Big drug deals going down in seventh grade?"

"Shut up."

Mom opens the back door and sets three huge lilies next to me on the seat. One pokes my face. It smells like a funeral. "Aren't these beautiful?" Mom asks. "The church let us have them for free!" Then she looks at our faces, which are the opposite of big beautiful flowers on Easter. "What's wrong? Are you two fighting?"

"No," Murphy says.

"No," I say.

"Good," Mom says, and slams the door harder than she needs to.

I want to glare at Murphy in the rearview mirror but I don't want Mom to see so I glare at the lilies instead, which isn't really fair, because they can't help it that humans designated them the death flower. Maybe in another dimension they're wedding flowers, and whenever people smell them they want to sing and dance and fall in love. And the wedding lilies think about the death lilies in our dimension and just feel sad for them.

Murphy turns in to the cemetery and we pass through the black gate and the gravel crunches under the tires. Like bones. "Home," I tell the lilies.

"What?" Mom says.

"Nothing."

Murphy rolls his eyes. He parks the car and we get out. The birds are chirping like they figured out what's going on at all the churches this morning and are just as excited as we are. *He is risen!* they tell us. *Hallelujah!* What a weird day to visit a cemetery. Jesus is risen but everyone else is still dead. But there's a bunch of other families doing it too. With their own pastel ties and church flowers and stomachs thinking about ham.

We carry the lilies to Dad's grave, one for each of us, and set them down next to the stone, which came in last week. It's basically the worst stone ever. It has three lines:

Lawrence Arthur Olson

November 23, 1950 – December 18, 1990

Beloved husband and father

That's it. No hearts or flags or even a little squiggly line somewhere. And the gray of the stone is—what's the word? Mottled. Like barf. Or soup. Or someone with the flu.

Mom arranges the lilies around the back of the stone. "I should have gotten one more," she says.

"Or one less," Murphy says, and Mom gives him a look that says, *If I could punch you in the face, I would.* "I'm going to wait in the car," Murphy says. *Hallelujah!* the birds chirp. He walks away. The car door shuts. Mom and I stare at the stone and the lilies, kind of like we stared at the cross on Friday. There's just nowhere else to look. The sun is buttery above us, climbing to its highest point. *He is risen!*

"Do you like the stone?" Mom asks.

"Yes."

We walk back to the car so we can visit Grandpa before the nursing home serves lunch at 10:45 in the morning. Murphy will pace in the hallway. Mom will open every drawer in Grandpa's dresser to make sure all the socks and shirts are clean. (They will be.) And I'll stare at the birds flapping around Dad's bird-feeders and say, "Look, Grandpa. A nuthatch."

■ ■ ■

I get to the library so early that it's only Jenni sitting on the "reading rug," which is not a thing that belongs in junior high, but tell that to Mrs. Peterson who says sitting on the ground in a circle "equalizes" us.

"You came!" Jenni says.

"Yeah." I drop my backpack onto a smiling green bookworm with bifocals. "I read the book, so . . ."

She nods. "What'd you think?"

I shrug. "Cool, I guess." I sit down next to her, and the air buzzes between us. I hope I'm wearing deodorant.

"And do you have a salient point to raise today?" she asks, in a perfect Mrs. Peterson voice.

"That's freaky."

"Thanks. I've been working on it for like two months." I picture Jenni at home, talking like Mrs. Peterson in the mirror, and laugh.

"Actually, I do have one," I tell her.

"Well done, young man. Let's have it," Jenni (Mrs. Peterson) says.

I find the page I folded down and read, "And when they heard the gun booming and saw the green flag fluttering at the masthead, their hearts swelled with imperishable pride."

Jenni's face turns back into her own.

"It reminds me of my dad," I tell the open book.

"Because as much as he hated the war, as much as he . . . suffered from it . . . he was still proud to be an American. I think. Like, he would tear up hearing the national anthem, but he never sang it. And we went to the parade every Memorial Day, but he never wore his uniform like the other guys."

Jenni leans toward me a little, so I can smell her shampoo. I take a deep breath. "When we buried him, we didn't even know if we should use the flag." I scratch at the hole in the knee of my jeans. "We did, though," I tell her. "We did use it."

Then I just run out of words and it's quiet around us. Quieter than any library ever, and that's saying something.

"That," Jenni whispers, "was a very salient point."

The rest of book club arrives and everyone drops their backpacks on the reading rug and Mrs. Peterson passes around the snacks and the air gets loud, but between Jenni and me it stays quiet, like a small secret, like knowing everything is made of superstrings.

• • •

"Hello. Are you a Skipper?" the parrot asks when I walk into the art room.

I blink at him. I'm the opposite of a Skipper. I've never even been on a sailboat. He means a Minnetonka Skipper, but can you even be that if you don't play sports?

Kyle lifts up the black hair that hangs down over his eyes, and says, "You don't have to answer him, you know."

"Oh. Right." I'd planned to just, like, slide into the art room and sit in the corner, but I guess not.

"Cheese and crackers!" the parrot says.

Kyle rolls his eyes, which have black makeup around them. "I hate whoever taught him that. It's so predictable."

I smile. Kyle and I used to be friends in elementary school. I guess we still are. I mean, we're not *not* friends. But when we got to junior high Kyle started wearing all black and painting his fingernails and listening to weird music, and I . . . I guess I just kept being the same.

"So, what are you doing here?" he asks. We're the only ones in the room, besides the parrot.

"I just, came to draw something."

"For a girl?"

I look down at my shoes and realize they're the same kind I've been wearing since fourth grade and feel predictable, like the parrot. I look back up. "How'd you know?"

Kyle shrugs and looks down at his drawing. "Lucky guess. Can you draw?"

"Kind of. What are you working on?"

He holds up his sketchbook, and it's the most amazing drawing of a tiny house on a hill but in outer space. It's all in pencil but it looks 3-D. It's weird but familiar at the same time. "Wow," I say. "That's so good. How'd you learn to do that?"

Kyle shrugs again. "Practice. I'm not happy with it, though. There's paper and pencils in that drawer." He points by tipping his head because he's already drawing again.

I get some paper and have to sharpen the pencil, which sounds like an auger in ice because the room is so quiet, but Kyle doesn't seem to care. I sit down a few stools away from him and for a long time it's just the sound of our pencils scratching and erasers erasing and the parrot whistling the Minnetonka Skipper fight song.

"So how's it going?" Kyle asks after a while.

I look up to see if he's talking about in general or with the drawing and luckily he's looking at my paper. "I don't know," I say, which would actually work for both questions. "I can't get this right." I'm trying to draw a flower for Jenni, which is so lame, and feels even lamer when Kyle comes over to see it. "I'm trying to make it seem like it's growing," I say. Lamely.

He nods. "Maybe some lines, like, going up here. Can I?"

"Yeah." I slide the paper over and he fixes it in two seconds. "Jeez. Thanks."

He nods and goes back to his stool. After a few minutes he says, "I like that. A flower growing instead of just sitting there in a vase."

"Thanks."

The parrot sings, "Spread far the fame of our fair name, and *fight,* you Skippers. Win this game!"

CHAPTER SEVEN

"I don't get it," Phuc says. "You're so good at English. Which is, like, words. How can you be so bad at this?" He's trying to explain (again) how to set up an equation from a word problem.

I shrug. "I really don't know."

The thing about Phuc is, he never gives up. Never. If Phuc ever gives up on anything, you better collect your valuables because it's definitely the apocalypse. He puffs one cheek up with air, then the other one, back and forth, thinking. Then he puts his pencil on one side of his desk and mine on the other. "Okay. This is point A." He taps his pencil. "And this is point B." He taps my pencil. "So this train leaves point A traveling at twenty miles an hour." His pencil chugs across the desk. Slow. Like an inchworm. About the speed of the trolley that killed Dad. "And this train leaves point B moving at thirty miles an hour." He pushes my pencil, faster. I picture a little plume of smoke coming from the point. I hear a train whistle. "So we have to figure out where they'll meet."

"That's impossible."

"No, it's not. You just have to know how to set up the equation."

I picture Dad at the edge of the lake. The trolley's coming and he's setting up the equation. The wind is a cold slice. The ice on the lake is eleven inches thick. The sky is black with white stars. The trolley moves in a colorful haze, full of glowing Christmas lights and bundled-up riders. To his right, the ladies at the hot chocolate stand are filling up the cups. Dropping a marshmallow in each one. He thinks, *If the trolley is traveling at twenty-three miles an hour and I step out at point A, is it fast enough to kill me?* He's squinting at the trolley. It's clattering down the tracks. He's ticking off the seconds.

Or not. Or he's looking at the lake and smoking a

cigarette and thinking misty, mystical thoughts full of green leaves and wet air and he turns around to cross and the timing's off.

"Phuc," I whisper. He pauses, midsentence. I didn't mean to interrupt him but I didn't realize he was talking. The pencils have met and stopped, not in the middle but at some random spot that Phuc knows how to calculate. "Do you think my dad killed himself?"

Phuc swallows. "I don't know."

"Me neither. But I need to find out."

"How?"

"I don't know. I asked Murphy to help me, but he won't. And I can't ask my mom, so . . ." I look away.

Phuc resets the pencils at point A and point B. "Why don't you go read the police report?"

"Holy crap!"

"Justin," Mr. Lindberg says. "Language."

"Sorry! I never even thought of that," I tell Phuc. "You're a genius!"

He shrugs. "My neighbor's a cop."

I want to hug Phuc, but that's not what we do, so I say, "Okay. Show me again."

He smiles, and the pencils start to move.

. . .

At the top of the STATE OF MINNESOTA DEPARTMENT OF PUBLIC SAFETY TRAFFIC ACCIDENT REPORT, there's a box labeled KILLED. It's in between VEHICLES and INJURED. And on this report, in the KILLED box there is one tiny little mark. What do they call those? Tally marks. Just one vertical line. One man. "That's him," I whisper to no one. "That's my dad." His whole life came down to this. One teeny mark, the length of a ladybug, on a single sheet of paper.

The report keeps blurring like my brain is refusing to focus on it, trying to protect me. Murphy told me something like that from his psychology class. Sometimes our bodies and brains just shut down, he said, to keep out the pain. When it's too much. But I keep blinking and forcing my eyes to adjust. I move my finger along the letters and numbers to keep them sharp, across Dad's name and address and birthday. He was born on Thanksgiving, and every year after we said grace, Grandma would stand up and say, "Larry, I'm so thankful for you! You are my Thanksgiving blessing!" even though Thanksgiving changes every year and was hardly ever on his birthday. And Dad would look shy but with shiny eyes. The way Murphy looked when Phuc's mom took us to KFC last week and Phuc and I made a big deal about waving to him at the fryer. (Sorry, Mom.)

There's not much here, really. Not much to protect me from. Just the approximate speed and driver response. I've imagined so much worse that I feel let down. I thought there'd be some kind of answer. Like the way Dad looked or maybe that he called something out. It seems stupid now. I read the report again. Nothing. Not even the stuff I told the police at the hospital about how much Dad drank, so I don't know why they asked me.

I stand up to leave, but then I see the list of witnesses. The first two I don't know. Most people in Wicapi have ridden the Christmas trolley a billion times and don't bother with it, but people come all the way from Minneapolis to ride it and drink crappy hot chocolate out of Styrofoam cups. They think it's quaint. *But not that day,* I think, and laugh. (What would Murphy's psychology teacher think about that?) But the third witness is Mrs. Florence Meyer. My third-grade teacher.

I don't go home when Rodney lets me off the bus. Instead I walk down Water Street with the lake and train tracks behind me. Past the pet shop and hardware store and library and bakery and comic shop and all the places in between. Past the Wicapi Welcome store that sells postcards with loons and lady slippers and Babe the blue ox on them. Past the empty space where they put up the Christmas tree, to the very beginning of Water Street, where you can take a right to Prince of Peace Lutheran Church (nope) or take a left to Wicapi Elementary. I go left.

Mrs. Meyer is at her desk grading papers, and the four o'clock sun shines across her in glittery stripes like golden guitar strings, and for a second I just want to leave her there, but I can't. I step into the room and the air is soft and the clock is ticking on the wall and it smells like pencils. The art project about March coming in like a lion and going out like a lamb is on the wall, and there are more lions than lambs. I chose a lion too, and I was super proud of how jagged I made his mane, but I might choose a lamb now. It's crazy that the last time I was here, Dad was alive, waiting for me to come home off the bus. But maybe he still is, tucked in one of Phuc's dimensions.

"Justin!" Mrs. Meyer says. "What a sweet surprise." She gets up and comes around the desk and hugs me. She looks smaller and older, with her white hair and button-up sweater. But it's only been a few years, so probably that's not possible. "How are you?" she asks.

"I'm good."

"Just here for a visit?"

"I, um, I came to talk to you, actually." I think I see panic pass across her eyes, like a random black wave between a bunch of gray ones on the lake, but it's so fast I could be wrong.

"Well, come on and sit. Can you still fit into these little desks?" She smiles, and we slide into two desks next to each other. She folds her hands on top of hers. I trace the pencil drawing on the top of mine with one finger. It's a Ninja Turtle. Pretty good one too. "That's Dylan's desk," Mrs. Meyer says. "He's a lot like you. Quiet, and smart." I'm silent. I know I have to ask, but I can't find any words. Mrs. Meyer tips her head toward me. "What did you want to talk about?"

I take a deep breath. "I read the police report," I tell her. "I saw your name, as a witness. The night my dad . . ." I'm looking down, talking to the Ninja Turtle. "And I've just been wondering. I just . . . need to know. What happened."

Mrs. Meyer breathes in slow like she's trying not to disturb the air around us. "Well, you read the report, right?"

"Yeah. I mean, I know what happened, basically, but the report doesn't say . . . It doesn't really say if it was an accident . . . or if he . . . like . . . stepped out . . . on the tracks." I look up at her now and she stares back at me. She taps her folded hands on the desk. Once, twice.

"You know, Justin, I can't say anything for sure."

"Okay."

"But it looked to me like your dad, well, he was just . . . lost in thought."

"Lost in thought?"

"I'm sorry. I know this is terrible for you."

"No, it's okay. I asked, so."

She nods. "He must have seen the trolley, of course, but his eyes were on the lake. Or on something . . . else. It happened so fast, really. I thought he would make it right across, and then he just . . . didn't. Almost like he . . ."

"Froze," I say.

She whispers, "Right."

. . .

Jenni runs up behind me in the hall and punches my backpack. I flinch, thinking it's Mitchell, and she laughs. "Jumpy much?" she asks.

I smile and shrug. "Yeah. I guess."

"Thanks for the drawing."

"Yeah, it wasn't that good."

She squishes up her face, which somehow makes her even cuter. "Are you kidding? It's perfect. I hung it up in my room."

"Really?" My heart is pounding in my throat, and please, God, don't let her see it pulsing in my neck like in an alien movie. "Kyle helped."

She tips her head. "Interesting. Soooo a bunch of us are gonna hang out at the beach on Saturday. You wanna come?"

"Isn't it kind of cold for the beach?"

She smiles in a way that makes me feel like a second grader. "Not to *swim*. Just to hang out."

"Oh. Like who?"

"I don't know, just people. Whoever. *I'll* be there!" She bats her eyelashes at me, then punches me in the shoulder.

What I say is: "Okay. Cool. I'll try to come by."

What I mean is: No way. Just the thought of that makes me want to jump in a deep hole and pull all the dirt over my head or move permanently to Mexico City. Possibly both. And I don't even speak Spanish.

Jenni shrugs. "Okay. Well, maybe I'll see you there."

"Yeah. Okay."

. . .

"Yes! Why did you get these?" There's an entire plate of pizza rolls, just for me.

Mom's sitting at the table with a beer, which she sips. "I have no idea. Moment of weakness."

I bite into the first one. It's been sitting for the

perfect amount of time and doesn't even burn my mouth. "Pepperoni. You're the best mom ever."

"Mmm." She turns the beer can around and around, like she's trying to see all sides of it at the same time. "Sergeant Swanson called me at work."

I stop chewing. Then start again, so I don't seem suspicious. "Oh yeah?" I say with my mouth full.

"I read him the riot act."

I sit back in my chair. "Are you serious? But he was so cool."

"Yeah. That's the problem. Who lets a twelve-year-old read a police report without parental permission? I have to sign a form for you to walk in the Halloween parade, for Pete's sake."

"So what'd he say?" I ask.

"A bunch of nonsense about how you had a right to know. Are practically a man, fathers and sons, blah, blah, blah."

I pop another pizza roll into my mouth, and the chemical pepperoni bursts on my tongue. I love pizza rolls. Even if Phuc says there's rat hair in them. I don't care. "I knew I liked that guy."

"Yeah, well. He likes you too."

"So why'd he call you, then?"

"The chief found out about it and made him."

"Oh. He's not in trouble, is he?"

Mom shakes her head. "I don't think so."

"Good. Want one?" I hold out a pizza roll on a fork, and Mom looks at me like, *Are you serious?* I shrug. "More for me." I stab another one and eat two at a time.

"Justin."

"What?"

"Why didn't you just ask me?"

"Ask you what?"

"About Dad. And the trolley."

"How would you know anything? You weren't there."

"I know *Dad.*"

"Mom. Did anyone really know Dad?"

Mom stands up and tips her beer up to get the last sip. For a second I think she might crush the empty can on her forehead, like in Murphy's favorite movie, *Animal House,* which came out the year I was born, so Murphy always says I'm the second-best thing about 1978.

"I did," she says. "And you did too." She kisses the top of my head.

. . .

My brilliant plan to pretend I thought it was the other Tuesday of the every-other-Tuesday—the one where I don't see the social worker—has failed. I was sitting perfectly happy in geography (or as happy as you can be in a class where you still use colored pencils) when the intercom buzzed and the secretary said, "Justin Olson to the main office, please." So instead of just being mysteriously missing from class, everybody watched me pack up my stuff and stare at my shoes until the door shut behind me.

At the office, the secretary's on the phone and nods toward one of the chairs outside the social worker's door. I sit down, and a few seconds later the social worker sticks her head out and says, "Do you mind waiting a few minutes today, Justin?" and disappears before I can remind her that she called me! She was holding one of the thirty-seven tissue boxes she keeps all over her office, which every other Tuesday I pretend are enemy soldiers. My only goal in that office is to not have to use one of those boxes, and so far so good.

The secretary gives me a butterscotch, and I watch the main office be the main office. A girl comes in to call her mom because she forgot her science poster for the second day in a row. She listens to her mom yell on the other end of the phone and twists the cord so tight around her finger that it turns purple. A skinny kid who used to ride my bus before they changed the routes comes in and stands at the counter without saying a word. "Forget your lunch money?" the secretary asks, and he nods, but they both know he didn't have it to begin with. She hands him a dollar.

A girl comes out of the nurse's office wearing sweatpants three sizes too big, with her head down so her hair hides her face. The secretary offers her a butterscotch and she takes it. "Thank you," she whispers, and walks miserably back into the halls.

"Justin?" the social worker says, and I jump. "Sorry about that. You ready?" The boy who needed the tissue box and extra minutes walks past. He's a hockey player, one of Brandon's friends who saved me from Mitchell and the wall.

"Hey," he says to me.

"Hey," I say back, and follow the social worker into her office. Before the door closes, the secretary winks at me, and for some reason, it makes my heart burst like a firework.

. . .

I have so much stuff on the Dakota I needed one of those triple poster boards for my project instead of the regular kind! It cost $4.23, and that's after Mom's work discount. When I lay the board down on Benny H.'s table in the nonfiction section and unfold it, it hangs off the edges. "Wow," he says. "Lot of space to fill."

"Yeah. But I got tons of stuff." I start pulling papers and pictures out of my folder and laying them down and moving them around and trimming them with my scissors. Benny H. watches.

"What do you think?" I ask when the board is full. I pull out my glue.

"Good, good. Maybe switch those two." He points. "For the flow of the story." I switch them. Then I start gluing and it takes forever, but Benny H. stays. He doesn't say a word, but every time I glue something down, he pushes on the board to keep it still, which is a very simple thing to do, but every time he does it I want to cry, I'm so grateful.

When I finish, I'm just going to say it: it looks totally amazing. "What's the title?" Benny H. asks.

"Oh. I don't know. How 'bout 'The History of Wicapi by Justin Olson'?"

Benny H. shrugs. "What about *'Mni Sota Makoce'*?"

"What's that mean?"

" 'Land where the water is so clear it reflects the sky.' "

"Really?"

"Truly. Truth."

"Why did they take off the *'Makoce'* part? That's the best part, about reflecting the sky."

"Because they didn't know any better. Or weren't paying attention." He looks out the window, where it's starting to snow in tiny specks. "And people like simple things," he adds.

"How do you spell it?" I ask. Benny H. doesn't know, but the librarian calls some librarian friend somewhere and gets the spelling, which makes me picture the map of the United States crisscrossed not by a bunch of highways but by a network of librarians, all calling each other on the phone during critical moments like this one.

I write the title across the top, and at the very bottom right corner I add: *Benny H. Wicapi, MN. 1991.*

"What's that?" Benny H. asks.

"I'm listing you. As a source."

He tugs on the bottom of his beard. "A source. Yes. I like that."

"I mean, you're the one who told me about the Dakota in the first place, and you sat with me all this time."

"Ha! Time." Benny H. waves his hand like he's swatting away time the way you swat mosquitoes. "I don't live in time. Slave to time. Trapped in time. No. I live outside of time."

. . .

"Wow. Nice," Murphy says, looking at my poster, which is standing up in the kitchen like it's a member of the family. "How are you getting it to school?"

I set my juice down. "Um. The bus?"

"Are you sure it won't get wrecked?"

"Sorry. You're Murphy, right?" I point at him. "'Cause you kind of sound like Mom." Murphy rolls his eyes. "It won't get wrecked. Rodney will let me keep it up front if I want."

"Who's Rodney?"

"The bus driver? Duh."

"Yeah, no. I'm driving you."

"Sweet."

Murphy carries my poster down to the car, walking slow like an old person. He tucks it into the backseat then shuts the car door slow too, like it's a sleeping baby. "You sure you don't want to put a seat belt on it?" I ask, but Murphy just smiles and shakes his head. He starts the engine.

We stop at the bakery even though we just had breakfast, and when I can't decide between sugar and glazed, Murphy lets me get both, which Mom would never do. "That's why brothers are the best," I tell him, and shove him for fun, but he doesn't shove me back.

We get to school and I tell Murphy to just let me out behind the buses, but he waits instead, his little beater car sputtering in between all the big yellow buses, until he can pull up right across from the front doors. I get out and get my poster out, *gently,* and lean back in before I shut the door. "Thanks for the ride. And the doughnuts."

Murphy gives me a smile that says: *I should be doing more for you.*

But what else is there to do? He already taught

himself how to change the oil in the car and make spaghetti sauce, and last week he even fixed the leak in the kitchen sink. And I can't even get my circuit to work in science class. You would not believe how much I want that tiny little bulb to light up.

. . .

I know the class has to clap for everyone, but it sounds so good anyway. I told them everything. About the seven tribes of the Dakota shooting to Earth as seven stars from Orion's belt and being born at the meeting of the Mississippi and Minnesota Rivers. I told about the black bear ceremony and the feast for the first wild rice, and all the things they did in season: hunting, trading, spearing pike, maple sugar, trapping muskrats, blueberries, turnips, medicine plants, and back to wild rice.

I told how in 1852 a tailor from New York and his friends formed the Wicapi Pioneer Association and started building houses all over Dakota land. I told how he wrote that Wicapi was filled with "the most beautiful growth of timber that the eye could wish to look upon, consisting of sugar maple, black walnut, butternut, white and red oak." And how those same trees became Minnesota's first cash crop. The class actually gasped then. Not because we really understand what a cash crop is, but because it's so weird to talk about how beautiful something is and then cut it down for money.

I told how the government rushed the Dakota into signing treaties and broke them anyway. I told about the six hundred burial mounds around Lake Minnetonka, and Spirit Knob, and how the Dakota tried to hold on to the lake, through all the treaties, but couldn't. Then I told how thirty-eight Dakota were hanged in Minnesota and two hundred sixty were sent to prison and seventeen hundred were forced into a concentration camp at Fort Snelling. Fort Snelling! The place we all went to on the fourth-grade field trip! Where people dressed like pioneers made tools and tapped trees for maple sugar and did not say one word about the Dakota.

I told the whole story. Exactly how it was. How it is. I told them all the things we never see. Even Mr. Sorenson is smiling.

Then Tyler squints even though he already wears glasses and sits in the front row and says, "Wait.

What's that last line on your reference list? Is that Benny H., like, the homeless guy in Wicapi?"

I look at Mr. Sorenson. He blinks at me. "He's not really homeless," I say, like it matters.

"Okay. But is he considered a reliable source?" Tyler asks. "I mean, Mr. Sorenson said books and encyclopedias, so I'm just wondering."

I want to beat Tyler up for implying that Benny H. is unreliable. "He knows a lot of history," I say to the floor.

"He also talks to invisible beings," Tyler points out.

I shrug. I set my poster on the stack and go back to my desk.

"No worries, Cease-Fire," Brandon says as I sink down in my chair. "I thought you did great. I mean, maybe Benny H. is secretly a medicine man."

"I highly doubt that," Tyler says.

"Shut up, Owly. We don't know anything for sure."

CHAPTER EIGHT

Mrs. Peterson is back from her Power of Poetry in the Classroom conference, and she has a million bad ideas. Today's is called Word Pairings. We all have to write two random words on two scraps of paper and drop them into a jar that used to hold animal crackers. Poor jar. We're not allowed to write swear words or body words or insult words or gross words or bathroom words. So now that's all we're thinking about. And "by the way" Mrs. Peterson is going to check them all. "Take your time," she says. "Be creative. Be complex. Be evocative."

"What's 'evocative'?" Sarah asks.

"It's a word that pulls something out of you," Mrs.

Peterson says. Then she glares at us like daring us to make the very obvious bathroom joke.

"Why are we doing this again?" Mike asks.

Mrs. Peterson smiles and takes a deep breath, like she's trying to hold on to the *Power of Poetry in the Classroom* as long as she can before we crush it. "Because interesting things happen when two disparate things meet."

"What's 'disparate'?" Mike asks.

"Different."

"Then why not just say 'different'?"

"Okay!" Mrs. Peterson says, picking up the jar. So I guess we're not taking our time after all. I write "button" and "walleye," which are not evocative but are the first things that popped into my head, and drop them in the jar when it gets to me. Then, after Mrs. Peterson checks all the words and replaces three, the jar comes back around and I pull out "wilderness" and "tangerine."

■ ■ ■

"You look miserable, butter bean," Mom says. She's at the stove making dinner, and I'm watching tiny drops of rice water escape from the pot and roll down the sides. The lid is bumping around like a kid who has to pee. It's making me crazy, watching that pot, but I can't look away.

"I have to write a poem about a tangerine wilderness," I tell Mom. "Or a wilderness tangerine. My choice!" I give her a sarcastic thumbs-up.

She dumps a can of cream of mushroom soup onto a pan full of hamburger meat. It looks like gray death. There's a word pairing for you.

"Says who?" Mom asks.

"Mrs. Peterson. We're doing word pairings. Evocative ones."

"Ah. Well, can't help you there. Dad was the word expert."

I glare at her back. "Dad. A word expert."

She turns around and stares at me, but I can't tell what kind it is. "Come stir this for me."

"I'm doing my homework!"

"Justin!"

I get up and take the spoon and she leaves the kitchen. *Mushroom gore,* I think, stirring. *Cow cluster. Bubbling gloom.*

"Here." Mom hands me a faded blue notebook,

the color of sky in April, when it's trying to power up. "Dad's poems," she says, like it's obvious. I stare at her. Mushroom gore drips onto the floor, and Mom takes the spoon back.

"What?" I whisper.

"I almost gave it to you the other night, when you said no one knew Dad, but it's all I have. I mean, of his words. To give you. And words are so important to you. And I didn't know how old you should be, or whatever, but it just seems like the right time, so . . . There you go."

A charge is running through my body like someone poured staples into my bloodstream. The top of the notebook has a bunch of paper clips in it that are holding little sections together. "What . . . are these?" It's hard to form actual sentences.

"Each section is a poem," Mom says. She turns the knob on the stove down, and I think, *Simmering slush.* "He'd write a bunch of drafts, you know, then copy out the final one on the last page. Then clip it all together." She lifts the lid of the pot and peeks at the rice. It gurgles at her. She shuts it. My mind is racing but also stuck. How is Mom still doing regular things like peeking at rice when Dad. Wrote. Poems? And I'm Holding Them.

"So like Dad, right?" Mom says, and I look up from the notebook, to her face, for some kind of clue. "So organized," she says slowly, like that explains everything.

■ ■ ■

I sit on my bed and open the notebook, carefully, like it might crumble into powder in my hands and blow away under my breath and I'll never know what Dad was trying to say.

Swivel

Nice to meet you, *hand extended. The words
Come from this man but I hear them from
The boy. Slim chest and straight,
Straight hair, he reached out his hand too
But not to me. To a grandmother, maybe,
A cousin gone before. There were so many
Possibilities, so many already dead.*

Then his hand dropped and his head
Swiveled before he crumbled
Into the mud. I didn't have time for words,
Like for Annie's goldfish. I said words for a fish
But not for a boy. I didn't have time.

His head swiveled just like this man's chair
As he turns to greet me. To offer a job
If I can only stop sweating. If I can only
Shake his hand, the real one
And not the other, turning, already, to dust.

Courage

If any one of us had not been afraid
To be called chicken, just think
What could have happened.
A domino effect, a string of paper
Soldiers, linking arms all the way back
To the chopper that let us down here,
Back to Grayson's wheat field and Whitt's
Overcrowded apartment and Bagley's
Cast net off a splintered pier. There would be no
Lemon sun soaking everything

So our memories are lit from all sides.
There would be no memories.
Only our clean, separate pasts
And our yellow bellies.

War Machine

I see it like a great big adding machine,
The kind they had at the hardware store
Downtown. You put in everything:
1. *Youth, patriotism, economics.*
2. *Half a face in the muck, eyeball dangling in*
   the socket.
3. *Pride of country, but more than that—pride*
   of town.
4. *Laughing in pitch-black because things are*
   still funny.
5. *27 civilians in a grass house. Lighting it.*
6. *Boredom, hours not in seconds but in*
   pounds.
7. *An old, barefoot man leading the way. His only*
   English words are fish *and* heaven. *It makes*
   no sense.
So you take it all back out and start again.

Accountable

There is nothing special about this moment
And there is also everything special.
You are on your belly, on your blanket,
Rolling into a patch of sunshine
And out. You are drooling on a toy rabbit.
I say your name. Justin. Which means:
Just, upright, righteous. You look up
And smile at me. And I see everything:
All the pain and joy and heartbeats
Of your life. The one I brought you to.
Dear God in Heaven, have mercy.

■ ■ ■

"Hey," Rodney says when I get on the bus after school. "You okay?"

"Yeah. Just tired." He nods like he doesn't believe me. I know because it's the same nod the social worker gives me every other Tuesday when I tell her I'm okay. Luckily, Rodney doesn't try to get me to join Grief Group. (Grief Group! I can't think of anything worse. Not even the actual Grief!) But today it's true. I stayed up past midnight reading Dad's poems over and over. I read them over and over and over. Except the last one. I didn't read it at all. Because like Mom said, that's all there is.

All day, walking through school was like walking through one of those paintings with all the bright colors and pictures that don't quite make sense. A bride with a goat playing the violin. "Saturated," the art teacher called it. "Figurative." Chagall, I think it was. Dad's poems are swimming all around me. All the images, overlapping, washing in at strange times and places. It's like living inside the moment when *The Wizard of Oz* switches from black-and-white to color.

I crash into an empty seat on the bus, shove up against the window and press my cheek against the cold glass. I close my eyes but the pictures keep playing on the inside of my eyelids.

Phuc sits down next to me and I open my eyes again. "Hey," he says.

"Hey."

"You look like crap."

"Thanks."

"So what's up?"

"Didn't sleep much last night."

"Me neither," Phuc says. He yanks a baseball hat out of his backpack and pulls it down low on his head, like he might just catch a few z's on the ride home to make up for it. "I stayed up too late watching a NOVA marathon."

I shake my head. "Of course you did."

"Did you know that a blue whale's heart is so big that you and me could swim through the arteries? Single file, obviously."

"Right. Obviously."

"So what were you doing all night?" Phuc asks.

"Having weird dreams, mostly."

"About what? Zombies?"

I laugh. "No zombies."

Phuc shrugs. "All my nightmares are about zombies. Human minds don't like the in-between, you know. That's why zombies scare us so bad. They're both dead and alive, and our poor tiny brains can't take it. Like Schrödinger's cat."

"Phuc. English. I beg you."

"It's a thought experiment, in quantum mechanics. You never heard of it?"

I stare at him. "I've never heard of half the things you say. You know this. Go on."

Phuc nods once, accepting this fact. "So a cat is in a box, right? With some poison. And the cat is either dead or alive. But you don't know which until you look into the box, so at one point, the cat is both dead *and* alive—like, in your mind, but also in the realm of possibility. But when you actually look in the box, the cat is either dead or alive. So the question is, At what point does reality become one thing or the other?"

I blink. Twice. "My mom gave me a notebook of my dad's poems," I tell him. "There's only five and I read four last night."

"So, you don't want to read the last one?" Phuc asks. The bus pulls away from the curb, chugging between the other buses, toward the street.

I look out the window. "I do want to."

"Are you afraid of what it will say?"

"No." The bus pulls onto the main road and picks up a little speed. We bump past all the houses we always bump past. Slush on the streets. Brown trees full of sticks, still far from spring. I look back at Phuc. "But I'm afraid of *knowing* what it says. Like, once

I read it, that's it. I won't know any more about him ever. This is the last piece of . . . evidence."

Phuc nods fast, the way he does in math when something clicks. (I never nod in math because almost nothing clicks, and if it did, I wouldn't be excited enough to nod rapidly.) "Exactly! That's what I mean, about Schrödinger. Once you look in the box, the cat is either dead or alive. There's no going back. That's reality."

■ ■ ■

"So what did you think?" Mom asks. She woke up early to fold the laundry before her double shift, which she and Murphy have been doing lots of lately. Murphy, who used to run after the garbage truck in his socks in the snow, laughing and holding up the white plastic bags, almost every Thursday morning. The truck would stop, of course. And the guys would roll down their windows and cheer and pump their fists in the air when Murphy tossed the bags perfectly into the back. Then Murphy would flex his muscles and bow to the empty street.

"About what?" I ask.

"Dad's poems." She tucks two socks together with this daydreamy smile, like maybe the socks are soul mates, and lays them on my pile. It's like she just asked a fairy-tale question and is waiting for an answer with the words "fate" or "true love" in it.

I think a lot of things. I think, *I was raised by a stranger.* I think, *Dad was an amazing writer.* I think, *Dad didn't trust me.* I think, *How did Dad make the inside of his head so beautiful?* I think, *Dad sucks for dying (possibly on purpose) so he can never answer any of my questions. And now I have a billion more.* I think, *I wish I never knew those poems existed.* I think, *Thank God I have those poems.*

I fold a towel, for something to do. Also because I don't really know how to fold anything else. Mom watches me for a minute, then asks, "Did you like them?"

"I guess, but . . ." I shrug.

Mom smiles, but barely. "I know a few of them are . . . tough." The coffeepot gurgles like it's about to throw up, and I can relate. Mom goes to pour her coffee. "But those poems are like a window into Dad's soul."

"A broken window."

She stops pouring, so her cup is half-full and the pot hangs in the air and the coffee sloshes backwards and she looks at me and her eyes have tears in them. I pick up my laundry and take it to my room and throw it on the floor.

■ ■ ■

I'm almost to my faraway point: the bottle Mr. Bauer painted on the wall in the science wing, with a lime-green chemical bubbling out the top. To be specific, my faraway point is the very top bubble, off on its own, like the wind might be blowing it. Or maybe the bubble is just happy to be out of the bottle, away from the crowd. But then I hear Jenni's voice say, "Justin will know!"

She's standing with two friends. I can't remember their names because she has so many and I've spent a lot of seventh grade avoiding them by staring at things like bubbles on walls. But Jenni is the opposite of me. Around her, everything fits. Her friends, the books in her arms, the lockers behind her, and Mr. Bauer's other drawings over her head (lightbulb, magnet, DNA, nuclear energy). And all the noise. Shoes walking, lockers banging, laughing. I think, *I will never fit into this scene.*

"He's *so* smart," Jenni says. She's waving me over with one hand. Her fingernails are painted pink. I step toward them, and the other two girls stare at me. "What comes first?" Jenni asks. "Order or family?" My head is full of dry sand, and so is my mouth. I know she's asking about science, but pulling those two words out confuses me. *Order* and *Family.* How can they be so plain and so important?

"Sorry. I . . ." I can't finish the sentence. Jenni's friends look at each other. Then one looks at the floor and the other one runs off to catch up with someone else.

Mom made up a little song before that test last fall, to the tune of "La Cucaracha." "*K* for 'kingdom,' *P* for 'phylum'!" I can see her dancing around the kitchen, shaking imaginary maracas. And at the same time, I see her holding the stopped coffeepot with tears in her eyes. Both Moms are in the kitchen, crossing over each other like ghosts. And now there are tears in my own eyes. Jenni's other friend drifts away and joins the stream of kids walking to the next class, like Mr. Bauer's top bubble.

So now it's just Jenni and me. The happy Mom, the one with the maracas, is fading from the kitchen. "Then comes class, order, family, genus, species!" I let the tears fall down my cheeks. I don't care. Or at least that's what I tell myself because I couldn't stop them if I tried.

"Order," I whisper to Jenni, who is now holding on to my arm. "Order comes first." I rub my eyes with the hard parts of my palms, like a punishment, and walk away. Mom shakes one finger and says, "Don't forget 'subphylum'! It is on the bottom!" and disappears.

■ ■ ■

It's my first time on the bench that I'm not looking for Benny H. and as a matter of fact, I hope I don't see him. I hope I don't see anyone. I stare at the frozen lake and try to make my mind gray and blank, like the ice. Like Phuc says monks do (real ones) when they meditate. So I can get a break from all the colors and words and that buzzing feeling like someone added extra blood to my body but there's nowhere for it to go. And from the last poem, still waiting for me. When should I read it? How long do I want Dad to last?

I'm staring so hard at the ice it takes me forever to hear the water.

I walk to the shore and bend down to the lake. The ice is out all along the edges and the open patches of water are blue, reflecting the sky the way the Dakota said it. I stick one hand in and the water is cold and clear. I stick in my other hand and stay like that for a long time, like time is irrelevant now, like maybe I live outside of time like Benny H., feeling my hands get colder and colder.

■ ■ ■

Luckily, Mr. Lindberg hands our tests back flipped over so no one else can see the red *C* at the top of mine. I've always sucked at math, but I've never gotten a C in my life.

"Justin," Mr. Lindberg says.

"Yeah?"

"Come see me a minute, before you leave."

"Okay." The rest of the class is packing up. Phuc already has his backpack on and both thumbs tucked into the straps, which makes him look like he's going into battle. Which he pretty much is, going into the halls with his hair gelled up like that. I shake my head quick, trying to clear it, but it's all cluttered up like an old nest, filled with leaves and feathers so you can't see the pattern anymore—the sensible circle it started with.

"You okay?" Phuc asks.

"Yeah."

"Hate to say it, but you *still* look like crap. Or maybe worse."

"Phuc," Mr. Lindberg says, all the way from his desk. "Language."

"Sorry," Phuc calls to him. "You sure?" he asks me, and I nod. He knows I'm not okay, but what's he going to do about it? What am I going to do? What is there to do?

I walk to Mr. Lindberg's desk and sit in the chair he pulled up next to it. I tuck my backpack between my feet, and it reminds me of Phuc's thumbs. We are all in battle. But not Mr. Lindberg. He has on a navy striped shirt and pants that look like they belong to a suit, like maybe he should be a businessman instead of a math teacher. His shoes have tassels, and his hair is gelled like Phuc's, but (reasonably) sideways. "I'm worried about you," he says.

"I'll study harder for the next one. I just . . . lost my focus."

But Mr. Lindberg frowns. "It's not the test. You don't look well. Do you feel okay? Did you sleep last night?"

I shake my head. Not last night. Or the one before that or before that.

"What's on your mind, Justin?"

I do not say, *I am being tortured by five poems in a notebook under my bed.* I do not say anything.

Mr. Lindberg waits. He's relaxed in his chair, like this is just another equation for him to solve. *Justin, a seventh-grade boy, recently lost his father in an unbelievably embarrassing accident. Well, was it an accident? Let's say "incident." So far, he seems to be doing well, but of late, he seems distracted and tired, and recently got a C on an exam. How do you (a) find out what's bothering him (other than the obvious reason stated above), and (b) offer a solution? Show your work.*

"Why do you teach math?" I ask Mr. Lindberg. "I mean, what do you like about it? I mean the math part, not the teaching." Because, seriously? There is no way he likes the teaching.

Mr. Lindberg smiles. "No one's really asked me that before." He drums his fingers on his desk. "I think what I like about math are the possibilities in it."

"Possibilities?"

"Yeah, like, the more we know about math, the more equations we have, the closer we get to the truth of things. Everything we know about the universe begins with math."

"Huh."

"But also." He sits up a little straighter. "There's this sense that we'll never know it *all*. We're just on this journey toward knowing. Then someone discovers something else and we get another piece of the puzzle. Or maybe we launch in a whole new direction. It's exciting!"

"'Exciting' is not a word I would have used."

He laughs. "Maybe not with algebra." He rubs his

cheek with one hand, like checking his shave, which is perfectly smooth, like everything else about him. "But the cool thing about math is that no matter how much information we have, there is always more. There will always be more."

CHAPTER NINE

On the bench at the spot where Dad died, I open the notebook, slide out the last paper clip, and turn to the last written-on page. Not because of that stuff Mr. Lindberg said about truth and possibilities and how there will always be more. I know this is the last poem, and that Dad is dead no matter what. But I am still alive.

On the lake, the ice is completely out and the water is celebrating. All the waves are tossing around with their white tops high-fiving, and for some reason it makes me want to read out loud. I guess seeing all that splashing and freedom makes it seem easy.

"Like a Man

Four days of running, holding on
To the back of a bright green bike
While Justin wobbles and cries. (He's too
  scared.
Murphy did it on his first try.)

I let go, and the bike drunk-weaves. Crashes.
Blood blooms from his lip and peeks
Between his teeth. He's screaming
And so am I. 'Calm down!'

We sit. I lift the handkerchief to his face
And taste Grayson's blood. Grayson's blood
In my throat and in my nose, so I smell it
With every breath. In my hair and in my sweat.

I sputter and cry (I'm too scared),
And the handkerchief comes back
Under my bowed head. Here, Daddy.
Forget what I said. I want him to be
Exactly this."

...

I ring the doorbell and Phuc's dad opens the door. The news is on behind him, making the whole living room blue, and the reporter says, ". . . Kurds in northern Iraq, calling it a massacre." Phuc's dad is squinting either from watching TV in the dark or the dead Kurds or wondering what I'm doing here at nine on a school night. Or all three. "Hi, Justin," he says. "Come in, come in. Is everything all right?"

I nod, still catching my breath from running four blocks in the cold and dark. "Is Phuc home?"

"Yes, Phuc is here. In the kitchen." His voice has all this air in it. Like the words float more than talk. Like flower petals falling to the ground, in no hurry. "Come," he says/floats, and I follow him, through the blue light, into Phuc's yellow kitchen, which is glowing like it's the center of the universe, smelling like cherries and dish soap.

Phuc is at the table with his three sisters around him and his hair in a million tiny ponytails. "Don't say a single word," he warns me. His sisters are laughing and dancing and shrieking as always, all with wet hair and pajamas and bare feet.

"Phuc is so pretty!" one of the girls says.

His mom sits next to him, grading papers. She slides her pen down a row of numbers and marks out number five with a single green slash. It's nice that she doesn't use red. "Phuc is a good sport," she says, and smiles at me, and I guess my heart is still in there somewhere because I feel it crack. *We used to be like this. A family.*

Phuc stands up and swats away his sisters like gnats, and we go to the roof. The chairs are still there and Phuc brings two blankets. "You want the telescope?" he asks, halfway out the window. I shake my head. We sit and build our little cocoons. The sky is clear and starry.

"The Dakota call themselves Star People," I tell Phuc. "Because they came down from the stars to be on Earth."

"Why?" Phuc asks.

"Why what?"

"Why did they come down? From the stars to Earth."

"I don't know. The book didn't say." Phuc always thinks of questions like that, from a different atmosphere. I stare up. What *did* the Dakota see on Earth

177

that made them want to leave the sky? Or maybe they didn't want to leave? Maybe they were chased down? Or maybe they were sent by some kind of force? Like, on a mission? Or maybe it was their destiny and they had to come? *Go back!* I want to yell at the sky, at the Dakota, at the stars shooting toward Earth, at history, at everything that's already happened and can never not happen. *It's a disaster down here!*

"Earth does look beautiful from space," Phuc says. "Very deceptive."

"I read the last poem," I tell him.

"Really? What was it like?"

"It was . . . It was actually amazing. They all were." Phuc smiles at the sky. "They were like looking at a single moment in time, like a millisecond, through a microscope. But connecting it to all these other moments and things. They were intense. And sad. And . . . beautiful."

"That's so cool. Your dad wrote poetry and you didn't even know."

"Yeah. But that's all there is. So. The cat is dead. In reality. And I still don't know if he killed himself. My dad, I mean. Not the cat."

Phuc looks from the sky to me. "I don't think

you'll ever know that," he says, in the quiet flower-petal voice that sounds just like his dad's. "I'm sorry."

"Yeah, I know. Thanks." Then we just sit for a while, like we always do, watching the huge sky.

■ ▪ ■

I heard the car honking, I just didn't think my mom could be so lame. So Sarah, who's best friends with Jenni and one of the most popular girls at school, has to tug on my sleeve and say, "Um, Justin? Isn't that your mom?"

I look up, and Mom is waving frantically like she did when I got home from visiting my Iowa cousins one summer. When I was eight. "Yep," I say. "That's her."

Mom keeps waving, even though we're looking right at her.

"Thanks," I tell Sarah, and cross between the buses. I head straight for the car and Mom finally stops waving. I get in and slam the door and glare at her. "Thanks for that."

"I didn't think you could see me," she says.

"Well, I definitely heard you."

Mom grins. "How was school?"

"Fine until *now*. What are you even doing here?"

"I got off early, so I thought we'd pick up Grandpa and take him out for pie." Except we can't go anywhere because of all the buses, so we just sit, with the heat blasting between us and me trying not to make eye contact with anyone, and Mom fixing her bangs in the little mirror in the sun visor.

"Mom?" She looks at me, like this might be a question she knew was coming but has no idea how to answer. "Why do old people like pie so much?"

She laughs and snaps the visor shut. "Beats me. Hey! It's Tuesday. How was the social worker?"

"Social."

She frowns. "You should give her a chance. She seems super nice."

The last bus rolls past, and Mom pulls out behind it. The kids in the back are looking at a magazine and don't look at us (small miracles). "She is nice. But she's always trying to fix something, and there's nothing to fix."

"Hmm."

I roll my eyes. Mom always says "Hmm" when

she's trying to get me to say more. She learned it from some speaker they had at parent night. The bonkers thing is that it works. Every time.

"It's like she has this idea about how I'm supposed to be, and I'm just not that," I say. "I'm just me. Like, Grandpa could still write music, you know. I know he could. But he just wants to watch birds and eat pie. Fine. And Benny H. used to be a history professor, and now he just wants to walk down the street and talk to old ghosts. Okay. Why can't they just do what they want and it's enough?"

Mom nods. "And what do you want?"

"I want you never to honk like a crazy person in front of my whole school ever again."

Mom laughs. "Done."

"Mom?"

"Yeah?"

"Thanks for everything."

■ ■ ■

Kids are pouring out of Mr. Bauer's class while he's still yelling instructions for the extra credit that no one ever does because it's basically an extra project. As soon as I see Jenni, I call her name, before I can chicken out and pretend I'm not waiting for her.

"Hey," she says, and we start walking together.

"Hey."

"You okay?" she asks.

"Yeah. I wanted to say sorry about the other day, outside science." I half smile at her.

"No worries." We keep walking. "I forgot to tell you, we missed you at the beach that day."

"Yeah. I'm sorry about that too. I just . . . Right after you asked me, I had to deal with some stuff. . . ." I stop talking because I sound totally stupid.

But Jenni shrugs. "It's cool. I get it."

Then all I can think of is Dad. How he used all his words on Mom. How he listened to everything she said. And how I will never know if he killed himself, but I am 100 percent sure that he loved Mom more than anything else in the whole world.

"Wait," I say, and stop walking. So Jenni stops too. We face each other. The kids behind us bump into us, then start walking around like cars around an accident. Some stare at us. I can feel it because I'm so used to it. "Can I be honest?" I ask.

"Why wouldn't you be?" She's squinting like preparing herself for something she doesn't want to see.

"It was super nice of you to invite me to the beach. Like, super nice. And I super appreciate it. If, that's, even a thing. It's just that, ever since the stuff with my dad . . ."

Her expression changes, adjusting to the seriousness, and she leans forward.

"I don't like talking about it," I tell her, "and I know your friends are cool and everything. I don't mean . . . I just didn't want to, get asked about it or get, like, gawked at. Anymore." My voice cracks on "anymore." I take a deep breath and pinch the crap out of my arm. *Don't cry, don't cry, don't cry, don't cry.* "And the other thing is, you don't have to invite me to stuff because you feel bad. Like, I'm okay. I have my own friends, and I'm really fine."

"You thought I invited you because I felt bad for you?" Jenni asks.

"I mean, I don't know. I just . . . I'm just saying."

"For the record, I invited you because I like hanging out with you."

"Okay." My voice sounds like Axl Rose, as a kitten. Most embarrassing moment in the history of this hallway. I should probably nail a plaque to the wall, right where we're standing.

"But I get what you're saying," Jenni says. She lowers her voice. "About the gawking. That's totally understandable."

"Really? Thanks." I shove my hands in my pockets. For no reason.

"So I have another idea."

"Okay." I feel like I just tumbled out of a dryer and landed on the Laundromat floor but I'm still soaking wet, like the dryer ran out of dimes. This girl. I swear.

"Do you like scary movies?" Jenni asks.

"I don't know. I haven't seen that many." Or any. What in *God's name* does she see in me?

"Me neither! But there's this super scary movie Sarah told me about called *Children of the Corn.* You want to watch it with me? Just you." She points her finger and lands it on my chest. "And me." She aims her thumb back at herself and grins, holding nothing back, like Murphy used to.

My chest starts blooming like it's growing a flower in the exact spot where Jenni's finger landed. I smile. "That would be amazing."

. . .

"Dude, what happened?" I ask, and slide into the front seat where only dorks sit, but I don't care because (1) I am a dork, and (2) Rodney apparently had some kind of breakdown. He cut all his hair off and looks like a baby squirrel.

"I'm getting married." Rodney flashes a huge smile, and I can't help it, I picture his cheeks full of acorns.

"So you had to cut your hair?"

Rodney laughs. "I didn't *have* to. I wanted to."

"I don't believe you."

He laughs again, like the whole world is just full of soap bubbles. "I *did*. Let me tell you something, bro. When you meet the right girl, you'll do anything. If Kimberly asked me to move to Florida and wrestle a gator, I would. No questions asked."

I touch my chest where Jenni made the flower bloom. But then I panic. "Wait. Are you still gonna drive the bus?"

Rodney laughs (again). "Are you kidding? I'm gonna drive the bus twenty-four–seven just to pay off the wedding!"

I actually sigh with relief. "Her name's Kimberly?"

"Yeah."

"Is she nice?"

Rodney sets his big hand on top of my head. It covers the whole thing. His thumb hangs onto my forehead. "She's *so* nice." He turns back around and pulls the door shut, but I hang over the seat with my chin on my hands, watching him drive. "I told her about you," Rodney says.

I pick my head up. "No, you didn't."

"I did! She loves animals, right? Like, *really* loves them. Takes in every stray that passes by. Once she even picked up an earthworm! Little dude was burning up on the sidewalk, and I thought, 'Oh, that's nice. She's going to put him in the grass.' Nope! She carried him home and made him a perfect earthworm habitat and nursed him back to health. It only took an hour, but she kept him three days, just to be sure."

I smile, half because I could listen to Rodney talk all day and half because he's going to have a nice wife.

"So anyway, now she's got this turtle, and he's been through something. I don't know what. Had a crack in his shell and kept his head in all the time.

All the time. I didn't even think he had a head. And you know turtles, they bite, so I kept my distance. But Kimberly's got him eating lettuce right out of her hand! She said he's resilient, and I said, 'He reminds me of this kid on my junior high route. Justin.'"

He takes his eyes off the road when he says my name, just for a second, to smile at me in the rearview mirror, and I look down so he can't see me blushing. I didn't even know he remembered my name.

"'He's had some bad luck in his life, but he's not giving in,'" Rodney says. "'He's resilient. Just like Zippy.'"

Now I laugh the soap bubble laugh. "Thanks, I guess."

Rodney nods.

"And congratulations."

Rodney points at me in the mirror. "Right on!"

■ ■ ■

"Goal!" Murphy yells, and shoots both hands in the air like he scored it himself. "Goal, goal, goal!" He lifts me up and shakes me up and down, and I'm laughing but my teeth are banging together, which is a very weird but somehow awesome feeling. "Goal!" Murphy yells again, and he starts high-fiving everyone around him he can reach. Even when everything kind of settles down, there's still an electric current in the crowd, and Murphy's bouncing on his feet like he's on a Pogo Ball.

"Can you believe these seats?" he asks, and his face is lit with everything—the white of the ice, and the lights, and the energy around us, and the white of the Ns on the North Stars' jerseys, and maybe even the white of the stars outside, because Murphy is channeling everything bright, like a magnet. Pulling light to him. Something inside him is lit up too, like how the Dakota turned from stars to people but must have still been partly stars. Murphy. My Star Person.

"They're so close," I say.

"I know! When Rob gave me the tickets, I had no idea they'd be this good."

"I still can't believe you brought me." I heard his shoes pounding up the stairs and when he burst into the apartment, yelling my name and holding up the tickets, I said, "Don't you want to take one of your friends?" And Murphy said, "That's exactly what I asked my boss, but he said, 'Murphy, I'm proud of you. I know you're dealing with a lot of crap, but you're keeping it together. You're on time. You do your work. You smile at the customers. You deserve this more than anyone else I know.'" Murphy ran a hand through his hair and looked at the wall then. He's not used to bragging on himself. "That's true," I told him, and he said, "Well, ditto all that to you, Monk."

Murphy reaches over and messes up my hair but keeps his eyes on the game. "You're my good luck monk. Gotta bring you."

It's third period already, and Murphy keeps bouncing on his invisible ball, turning circles sometimes, change jingling in his pocket, whispering, "Just gotta hold 'em." I keep my hand around my green rabbit's foot in my coat pocket. I grabbed it from my sock drawer at the last second.

Then, the buzzer.

"We won?" Murphy looks at me, stunned. The score's been 3–1 the whole period, but Murphy really is surprised, because he stopped expecting anything good since Dad died. I know because I've been doing the same thing. "We *won!*" Murphy says again.

"We won!" I tell him, nodding. "We totally won!"

"We won! We made the playoffs!" Murphy yells. He lifts me up and shakes me again, and he's laughing and I'm laughing, and the whole stadium is laughing and cheering and jumping in a big happy roar. We've all been losing all season. Murphy, me, the North Stars, the fans. And now we're all—what's the word? Incredulous. Everyone is hugging and jumping and pumping their fists in the air and spilling their beer. Murphy's shaking his head, still unbelieving, grinning at the players circling and waving and scooping up flowers from the ice.

The goalie tosses the puck into the stands, and time does this weird thing. It slows down, but not like slow motion, just like a freeze, a stillness. So I can hold it in my mind. Preserve it. And I understand why Dad wrote poems and Benny H. lives outside of time and Mr. Lindberg says we will never know everything. Because who could have predicted this? What mathematician could have looked at these stats—all the lost games, Dad's body lying limp in front of a trolley, Mom counting pills on a bad ankle, Murphy frying chicken instead of playing baseball, and me getting pinned to the wall like a dead butterfly—what mathematician could have looked at all that and said, "*Win.* I predict a *win.*"

Then the moment speeds past and I cheer for the North Stars too, because tonight, it's not so bad to be on Earth.

CHAPTER TEN

On the front page of the *Star Tribune* there's a color photograph of Kurdish refugees on the side of a mountain in northern Iraq. They're so packed together that at first I think they're part of the mountain, like some kind of flower or grass. I read the article underneath, about where they're going and why, but nothing sinks in because I can't stop staring at that picture. Every time I look at it, I'm surprised that people can stand that close together and still move. That people can look so much like part of the landscape. We never learned anything like that in art class.

I'm still staring at it when Mom comes into the kitchen. "Hey," she says. "You still here? You'd better hustle or you're gonna miss the bus." So I tear out the picture, gently, and Mom watches but doesn't ask why, just like she didn't ask why when I begged her not to cancel the newspaper last week. She just said into the phone, "You know what? Just keep it like it is. I changed my mind." Then she hung up and smiled at me.

The bus is pulling up when I get to the corner, out of breath. I'm the last one on, and Phuc is the second-to-last because he was waiting for me a few steps from the bus stop, toward my apartment. It's the kind of thing I notice now—the space between me and other people, if someone turns away or steps closer, and how they stand. Or if they're like Phuc, who stands with me like he always did. We get on the bus and all of a sudden I realize Phuc probably waited in that spot, a few steps toward my apartment, through all those frozen weeks in January until I finally showed back up, and he nodded at me, like always.

We sit down, and Phuc takes the picture out of my hand. "What's this?"

"Kurdish refugees."

"Whoa."

"Yeah."

Phuc studies the picture. "It makes me wonder about my parents," he says.

"Really?"

"Yeah, because they never told us how they got here. Like, to this country."

"You're kidding me."

Phuc shakes his head. "You know how Mr. Bauer still uses that old slide projector?"

"Yeah."

Phuc keeps talking to me but looking at the picture. "And how when there's a slide missing the screen goes white until he clicks to the next one? That's like my parents. There's all these pictures of their childhoods in Vietnam. Then a picture of them standing next to the university sign in Saigon. Then a blank white space. Then a picture of their first winter in Minnesota. They were so cold. There's a picture of my dad standing in the snow with no coat on, holding up one foot to show off his new boots." Phuc laughs. "Super lame moon boots, but he loved them. He's told me a billion times about buying those boots." He hands the newspaper picture back to me. "But nothing about the white space in between."

"My dad never talked about Vietnam either,"

I say. I never thought about Phuc's dad being like mine. About them having the same white space, in between, in Vietnam. Were they on different sides, or not really? Mr. Sorenson said there were actually all kinds of sides. "History is more like a prism," he reminded us, "than a piece of paper."

What would've happened if our dads had met? Like, really met. More than nodding to each other at parent night or in the hardware store. Or maybe they never really met on purpose. Maybe they looked at each other and knew that all the missing pieces had to stay in the white space, where nobody could find them.

■ ■ ■

When the principal calls my name at the assembly, I don't hear it because I'm thinking about this: What if Phuc's dad and my dad actually crossed paths in Vietnam? Like, what if they walked right by each other in the street? And what if at that moment they looked at each other, just for a second? And what if a bunch of years later they passed each other at Wicapi Elementary and did the same thing? Is that what déjà vu is? Just the universe connecting you to yourself in another dimension?

Kenny Olson elbows me in the ribs. "Dude!" he says. He's grinning at me, and I never noticed before how many freckles he has, or how they look like stars tossed across his face. And I wonder why people make fun of freckles when they look so cool. "That's you!" Kenny says, and jabs me again. "They called your name!"

"For what?" I whisper, and Kenny laughs.

"National History Project. You won for the whole district. You're going to State!" He slaps me on the back. "Congratulations!"

I stand up at the very same moment that Brandon stands, shoots his fist into the air, and yells, "Cease-Fire!" which punches a bolt of happiness through my body that makes me laugh out loud. My legs are noodles like when Mitchell held me against the wall, but in a good way. I make it up the stairs, and the stage lights are five hundred degrees. Principal Berglund shakes my hand. His face is huge and bright like the white-flower moon, and his handshake is firm the way Dad taught me to do it. "Congratulations, son! So proud of you!" he booms, a human bass drum.

Someone takes a picture, and I look out and see

all the faces turned to me, smiling. All the hands are clapping, and all these people, everyone in this whole lunchroom that still smells like green beans, are cheering. For me. I can see Jenni nodding and Phuc giving me the thumbs-up, and Mom standing in back in front of the windows with her red pharmacy vest on and her cheeks pink like she just ran in, just made it. And Murphy's next to her, waving and whooping more than he did at the North Stars game, which I didn't think was possible. The afternoon sun is behind them, lighting up the edges of their hair, so they look like the angels in the children's Bible Pastor Steve gave all of us on first communion.

I walk to the podium and Mr. Sorenson hands me my certificate. "Congratulations, Justin," he says. "Well done." I turn to go back down the steps, but Mr. Sorenson says "Hold on a minute" into the microphone, and everyone gets quiet. "I have a confession to make. When Justin first told me his topic, I had doubts. I wasn't sure if it fit the criteria. But this young man turned in the most detailed, well-researched National History Project that I have ever seen in my seventeen years at this school."

The audience goes crazy again, and I look at the

floor. I don't know where else to look! It's too much! And Mr. Sorenson keeps going! "And Justin's project also reminded me of one very important thing. And that is, how critical it is to know our own history. To know our own land and our own people. All of the people who have called this place home. His project reminded me of how powerful that knowledge can be, and how lost we are without it. So I wanted to take a minute to say thank you to Justin." I look up, and he smiles, perfect white beard, eyes twinkling, history-teacher-Santa-Claus. "Thank you for taking a risk on this project. And for reminding us to honor the history all around us, every day."

. . .

I've biked up and down Water Street twice, and through a bunch of side streets. I went down by the beach and up the hill by the playground and back to the softball field, and past the corner bar and glassy apartments and paper shop where Mom got Dad's stationery for his grocery lists. I circled the bench and the train tracks. I've been to the library and the bakery, and now I'm back at the library.

"Still didn't see him?" the librarian asks, and I shake my head. She waves me over, and when I get to the desk, she whispers, "You know where his sister lives?"

"No," I whisper back.

She looks around. "I'll give you the address because I know you're friends, but don't share it, and you didn't get it from me."

I nod, fast, like Phuc when he solves a math problem. "Thank you so much," I tell her.

She writes it on my hand with a pen, and it turns out Benny H.'s sister lives only two blocks away, in a little white house with a bright blue door that I've passed about five million times in my life. The doorstep always has tons of pumpkins on Halloween, representing every human/pumpkin emotion. I knock, and a woman answers who is better dressed than Benny H. and a little older, but has the exact same green algae eyes.

"Hi. Um. My name's Justin, and I was looking for Benny H.? I wanted to give him this." I hold up my National History Project certificate.

"What is it?"

"It's . . . a certificate." But it doesn't look like it did

in the lunchroom. It looks like a piece of paper with a gold sticker. Like they gave us in elementary school for perfect attendance. "It's for a project he helped me with, and I just wanted to . . . give it to him."

She looks at me the way Benny H. does, like she sees not just the outside of me (open coat with broken zipper, hair that needs to be cut, Murphy's old sneakers one size too big), but everything inside too. All my blood and thoughts and dreams and past and future and connections to the universe. All the superstrings holding me in this spot. But it's not the kind of look that makes me squirm, like when Mrs. Peterson asks me for a *salient point*. I don't even look down. I just look back.

"Come on in," she says.

Benny H. is sitting on the couch. His lips are red and chapped and his forehead's pale without his hat, and for some reason, inside the house he looks so much older. He looks like an old man. He's looking at the wall, at a spot where nothing is, muttering a little. "Benedict Henry. Someone here to see you," his sister says, her hands on my shoulders. "Go ahead," she tells me, and I walk toward him.

Benny H. turns. "Hey!" he says. Then he coughs and coughs. His sister steps forward, but he waves her back and she disappears into the kitchen. I wait, frozen. He keeps coughing and spitting into his handkerchief. "Sorry, sorry!" he booms, too loud, like he's using his voice to prove himself. "What have you got there?"

I hand him the certificate, and he tips it toward the window to catch the fading light. "I won," I tell him. "For my National History Project. The one on the Dakota. I won for the whole district. I'm going to State."

Benny H.'s eyes shine. "You did it. Wonderful! Wonderful, wonderful." He shakes his head. "But I'm not surprised. You're a smart kid."

"Yeah, well. I had a good teacher."

Benny H. laughs his Jolly Green Giant laugh, then coughs some more. He tries to hand my certificate back, but I say, "Keep it. I wouldn't have gotten it without you."

He smiles at me, the big one where I can see the gap in his teeth, and my brain freezes this moment too, like at the North Stars game, so I'll have it later, when I need it. "Thank you," Benny H. says. "I will cherish this. I surely will."

. . .

"I just don't get how you can order strawberry when there's chocolate," I tell Murphy. "Or cookies and cream. Or anything that tastes like anything better than strawberry."

Murphy shrugs. "I like strawberry. Besides, I'm paying, so quit complaining."

"Good point."

We sit on the bench with our backs to the ice cream shop and our fronts to the movie theater and the lake and the park. We're at the corner of the whole town. The sun is weirdly strong for April, and everyone's in shorts with their pale legs hanging out, wearing sunglasses and smiling. Even the dogs look happy. I take a deep breath and try to suck it all in— the sunshine, Murphy next to me, the blue water and white waves, and the old ghosts too.

On the bench next to us, a dad is sitting in between two little girls, telling jokes, and they're shrieking with laughter, like Phuc's sisters. The dad kisses one on the forehead. He brushes her hair back under her headband with his thumb.

"Murphy?" I ask.

"Dude. Lay off about the strawberry. It's good. I like it. Just enjoy the moment, man." Murphy's wearing sunglasses with shiny orange lenses and has picked up the habit of saying "man" all the time. I think it's because a new kid from California started working at KFC. Murphy also now says he's *stoked* when something's awesome and stopped cutting his hair, which is so long it's curling at the tips.

"It's not about the strawberry," I tell him. "Which is not good. But whatever. It's about Dad."

Murphy doesn't change his expression. At least I don't think he does. I can't see his eyes, so it's hard to tell. He licks his ice cream. He's sitting back with his right ankle propped on his left knee. *Chilling,* he would say. "What about him?"

"Do you ever feel cheated?" I ask.

"By Dad?"

"No. By life. Or, not life, really, but by Vietnam. Like, Dad could have been a regular dad. He could've told us stories or given advice or . . . I don't know, guided us somehow. And he never got the chance. Doesn't that make you mad?"

"Did I tell you I'm taking psychology?" Murphy asks.

"Only one billion times."

"So there was this one study where they asked a whole bunch of people, 'Would you trade your situation for someone else's?' Like, if the other person had more money or a bigger house or a better job or whatever. And you know what?"

"What?"

"Most people said no." Murphy licks a pink drop spilling down his cone. "I forget the percentage. I'm not a brainiac like you."

"Ha ha."

"The point is, most people stuck with what they had. Because even if someone has more money or whatever, you never know what kind of problems they have on the inside. So if some scientist in a white coat came up to me and was like, 'Hey, Murphy, would you like to swap your Dad with a guy who talks and watches fireworks on the Fourth of July and doesn't walk in front of trolleys?' You know what I'd say?"

I shake my head.

"I'd say, 'Hell, no.' I get what you're saying about the stories and whatever, but that's just not the cards he was dealt. And in the end, we all just do the best we can with what we've got. And yeah, he wasn't perfect. Yeah, lost opportunity, whatever. But he did guide us, in his own way. There's a lot you can do without talking. You can play catch. You can play Scrabble."

I look away, and Murphy waits for me to look back.

"And he loved us," he tells me. "You know that, right?"

"Yeah." I look at Murphy with his crazy sunglasses and messy hair. "You know something, Murph?"

"What, Monk?"

"You're smarter than you look."

He laughs. "Thanks. That actually means a lot, coming from you." Then he smashes his cone against mine and leaves a big pink smudge on my perfect double chocolate.

We sit for a few more minutes, crunching through our cones, watching the lake that's been here, will be here, forever and ever, water, ice, water, ice, water. "Murphy?"

"Oh, God. Another deep question?"

"No. I just want to know if the North Stars have a shot." They just shocked us *again* by winning their first playoff game. Murphy actually kissed the TV screen at the buzzer.

"Probably not. Saint Louis is pretty sick."

But I smile because right now we're still in between, like the dead/alive cat. They *could* win. It's possible.

. . .

Mom's sitting at the kitchen table with her coffee and the Sunday paper, which I have never seen her read in my entire life. The sun is up somewhere, I guess, but not here. The curtains are open, but the sky is so full of clouds the apartment's a shady gray that makes it creepy, like someone's about to jump out of a closet. It's like yesterday—with Murphy, eating ice cream on the bench in the sunshine—never happened. I want to tell the universe, *No take-backs,* but the universe doesn't listen to me (obviously).

"Morning, butter bean," Mom says.

"Morning. How come you're not at church?" I sit

down at the table and tuck my feet under me to keep them warm.

Mom shrugs. "I don't know. I just woke up and . . . didn't feel like it. You want some breakfast?"

"Not yet. It's freezing in here."

"I know. I just heard the heat click on." She turns a page of the newspaper, but she's not really reading it. Her eyes are wandering around the pages. Then she says, "April twenty-first!"

"What about it?"

"It's my granny's birthday." She smiles and closes the paper. "We should plant some flowers in her honor."

I raise my eyebrows. "Seriously?"

"Yes. She had the most beautiful garden."

"Yeah, well." I toss my arm toward the window. "Pretty sure they'll die out there."

"We should ride our bikes," Mom says, like she didn't even hear me.

I sit up straighter. "Mom. Please don't go crazy. I need you. I only have one parent left." I'm only half kidding about this.

Mom laughs and looks right at me. Her eyes are a deep, dark brown. They're tired, but normal. Thank

God. She messes up my hair, then stands up and carries her coffee cup to the counter. "Justin," she says. "You can't wait for everything to be just right or you'll wait your whole life. Get dressed. I'll buy you a doughnut."

I yawn. "Okay, in that case."

. . .

My fingers are numb on my handlebars, and the wind is kicking up. The fern in Mom's bike basket is waving its arms around like a panic attack. "It's a little early for flowers," the woman at the nursery said, frowning at Mom. "We can get a hard freeze all the way to Memorial Day." And I wanted to punch her.

But Mom just smiled and said, "Well, what've you got?"

My ears are plugged with cold so all I can hear is gravel under our tires and tree branches shaking in the wind, and I can't remember being this happy.

We turn off the bike path onto Water Street, where we live. Where everything is. Where at the very end, Dad killed himself or didn't, and the lake is crashing into itself over and over. Mom tilts her head to the left when we get near the bakery, because I couldn't hear her if she tried to talk. We slow our bikes down and park them in the alley so the wind won't knock them onto the sidewalk. The screen door to the bakery is blowing around, and I catch it and hold it so we can walk inside. Mom is carrying the fern. I guess she figures it needs a rest too.

The air is full of sugar and yellow light and stillness. "Hey there," Joseph says. He's the owner and has a bald head and glasses and a friendly smile, and an apron full of flour and one stripe of pink jelly across the front. I grin at him because he's the one who gives Benny H. coffee and a doughnut for free every morning, and I can't think of anyone I love more (besides Mom and Murphy) at this second. "Sorry about the door," Joseph says. "I should just prop it open, but I like the drama of that breeze." Mom smiles like she knows exactly what he means. "Pretty fern," Joseph adds.

"Thanks," Mom says.

I order a chocolate doughnut and Mom gets glazed, and we sit with the fern on the little table between us, in no hurry, in the gold-leaf light, while Joseph chats with the customers, some coming from church and some not, and the door bangs and bangs in between two worlds, and it reminds me of the Dakota being created at the meeting of two rivers, like Mom and me being created at the meeting of street wind and bakery light. It's the kind of moment that Dad would have protected in a poem, and the kind that super-strings will repeat and repeat and repeat, without us even asking, after we leave.

A NOTE FROM THE AUTHOR

One of the best things to come out of my first book, *Once You Know This,* was being invited into middle schools to talk to kids about writing. To hear all of your beautiful, inventive ideas and insights, and to watch you create your own writing, especially when you didn't think you could.

I love that writing is accessible to all of us, no matter who we are or where we live. Because ideas are everywhere, all around us, all of the time. So if you want to be a writer, or any kind of creator, my best advice is to BE AWAKE and to BE CURIOUS. Pay attention to everything around you, no matter how small it may seem. Poems and stories often begin with a single thought, or image, or phrase, or connection, and bloom from there. As Mark Twain wrote, a writer "can only find out what [the story] is by listening as it goes along telling itself."

That's how this book began. I knew only that the main character would be a boy struggling with something that set him apart, and I was curious to see where it would lead. As I began to write, other characters stepped forward, the setting and time appeared, and the details sharpened. I did research Minnesota history and read books about war to give the scenes depth and color. But when I wrote, I simply imagined myself as Justin and walked through his world, which materialized as we went, almost as if he were creating it himself. Writing feels like magic in this way, because the story comes both from some other plane and from my own history.

Now that it's out in the world, *Like Nothing Amazing Ever Happened* has a life of its own. It doesn't belong to me anymore, which may be the most magical thing of all: stories can mean different things to different people at different times, and those things can all be true. This story now belongs to you, and you get to decide what to take from it, and what it means.

In addition to writing, I love dance. And one of my favorite quotes comes from Martha Graham, a dancer and choreographer who reshaped dance in the twentieth century. She said:

> There is a vitality, a life force, an energy, a quickening that is translated through you into action, and because there is only one of you in all of time, this expression is unique. And if you block it, it will never exist through any other medium and it will be lost. The world will not have it. It is not your business to determine how good it is nor how valuable nor how it compares with other expressions. It is your business to keep it yours clearly and directly, to keep the channel open.

I am convinced that all of us have a creative spark, whether it's expressed through dance or writing or inventing or painting or building or singing or some other way. I hope that you will have faith in yours, will rest assured of its uniqueness and importance, will cultivate it and trust it. I hope you'll keep the channel open. And I can't wait to see what you'll do in the world.

ACKNOWLEDGMENTS

As always, so many family and friends (and strangers) to thank. I am the sum of everything you've taught me.

Most of all, to Andre, Stan, Andrew, Leo, and Ila. You are the center of my world, and being with you is better than everything. Every day, I'm amazed at my luck, to hear the front door close behind me and your voices from every direction.

Thank you to Mom for tracking down all the history books and making friends with all the librarians in the process. (For teaching me how to move sweetly and strongly in this world.) To Dad for taking me ice fishing as a very little girl. (For teaching me to use the depth finder, on the lake and in life.)

Thank you to Corby Baumann for being my touchstone and source of hockey terminology. (Watching you play hockey is my proudest junior high memory.) To Ashley Cauley, honestly, just for being you: my coffee bean and sea ghost. And to Regina Benjamin for insisting (vehemently, repeatedly) that I trust my voice. And to Joy Lamar and Jenny Langhinrichsen-Rohling for being steadfast sources of encouragement and light.

Thank you to Wendy Loggia and Audrey Ingerson for growing this book in all good ways. I'm still stunned that I have this opportunity at all. And to Dan Burgess and April Ward for the beautiful art and design.

Thank you to Tim Mulcrone for your research and remembrance of 1991 police protocol. To Lisa Stevens with the Excelsior–Lake Minnetonka Historical Society for the excellent sources. To Dr. Katherine Hayes at the University of Minnesota for pointing me toward Dakota history. To Gwen Westerman and Bruce White for their invaluable book, *Mni Sota Makoce: The Land of the Dakota*. And to Tim O'Brien for *The Things They Carried,* David Finkel for *Thank You for Your Service,* and Sebastian Junger for *War.*

ABOUT THE AUTHOR

Emily Blejwas grew up in Excelsior, Minnesota, where she learned to ice fish and love the North Stars. She now lives in Mobile, Alabama, with her husband and four children. She directs the Gulf States Health Policy Center in Bayou La Batre. Her first novel, *Once You Know This,* was a Junior Library Guild selection that *School Library Journal* called "a poignant and emotionally driven debut."

EMILYBLEJWAS.COM